Pink or Black

∿

At the Lawrence School, Sanawar (a boarding school set in the sylvan Kasauli Hills), Tishaa's creative engagement was limited to penning down her daily diary. Just like all teenage girls, collecting Barbie dolls was like a mission in her life, but later bookstores ended up conquering the number one position in her list of obsessions. While her teen buddies were busy batting eyelids and breaking school rules to sneak out for a date, Tishaa began writing her diary. At the age of sixteen, she decided to pick up interesting incidents from that very diary to pen her debut novel – *Pink or Black*.

After a few character building years in a famous acting school and in dance academies, Tishaa finally realised that her passion and inspiration lies in the written word. She wants to become a story teller and plans to join the New York Film Academy to do a course in film making.

Pink or Black

Tishaa

Rupa & Co

Copyright © Tishaa 2008

First Published 2008
Fifth Impression 2009

Published by

Rupa . Co

7/16, Ansari Road, Daryaganj
New Delhi 110 002

Sales Centres:

Allahabad Bangalooru Chandigarh Chennai
Hyderabad Jaipur Kathmandu
Kolkata Mumbai

All rights reserved.
No part of this publication may be reproduced, stored in a retrieval system, or transmitted, in any form or by any means, electronic, mechanical, photocopying, recording or otherwise, without the prior permission of the publishers.

The author asserts the moral right to be identified as the author of this work.

Typeset in Baskerville 11 pts. by
Mindways Design
1410 Chiranjiv Tower
43 Nehru Place
New Delhi 110 019

Printed in India by
Rekha Printers Pvt. Ltd.
A-102/1 Okhla Industrial Area, Phase-II
New Delhi-110 020

ACKNOWLEDGEMENTS

For Mom, Dad and my brother Shaunik
My friends Shriya, Rhea, Bushra, Taaneya, Shivani and Safina
and
The Lawrence School, Sanawar
'Never Give In'

ONE

It was really so ironic! When Tiana finally got what she had wanted the most, she soon realised that she had changed as a person from the time she had wanted it. Now, she was not even sure if she actually wanted it at all!

The reason was clear; she could have been dead right now, but she had survived.

Now she sat in her bedroom, trembling with nervousness, hugging her pillow for consolation and staring out of the window. 'Snap out of it!' she told herself sternly. She wanted to forget everything, but the more she tried to push away those horrid thoughts, the more they haunted her. Somehow she felt guilty for having been lucky enough to survive. But then she realised that the real reason behind her survival was not luck . . . it was choice.

Almost four months ago, Tiana had been enlightened by the fact that the power of choice always existed. The choice could be between anything . . . it could be between truth and lies, right and wrong, and even between losing it and finding it . . . and she had decided, or rather chosen to find it. To understand what she was trying to find, you need to understand why she was trying to find it . . .

∫

Four years ago, she had metamorphosed from a loner and an awkward teen into the one of those members of the 'cool crowd'.

We all know the meaning of 'cool crowd' don't we? They are that one particular attention-seeking gang which is always considered cool, always having their own version of fun (or making fun of others), were friends with seniors (and we know that helps!) or were the favourites of the teachers. Whatever they wore was considered to be the 'in' thing of fashion. Whether it was half torn jeans that hadn't been washed for centuries or rags over your body . . . it didn't matter. If they wore it, it was no less that French couture! The lingo they used was the lingo that everyone else had to use and understand . . . if you didn't, God save you! If you did . . . well, you can consider yourself to be lucky enough to be one of them. That is precisely what Tiana had always wanted to be – 'cool' . . . and not a loser. Heck, isn't that what every school going kid wants to be? But she was lucky enough to cross over. Not every one manages that.

However, to be considered cool was not the main reason behind her desire to be part of that gang. The real reason was to protect herself from 'the gang' itself.

Tiana had been very excited at the prospect of going to study in a boarding school. Most of the kids in her previous school had laughed at her enthusiasm when she had confided in them. They told her that it would be like living in jail; the food would be awful and she would not even have a proper bed of her own.

Well, you can't blame them . . . that is exactly the kind of picture that is painted into the average kid's mind—nightmarish, cut off from the joys of life and imprisonment! Tiana understood where their fear stemmed from. They were scared of boarding schools because parents usually threatened to send their kids to one if they didn't behave properly. Tiana's case was different. Thanks to the long and frank talks that she had had with her parents, she knew what she was in for and that going to a boarding school was going to be nothing less than an adventure.

At the age of ten, she found herself gazing at the beautiful Hill View High. Set on a hilltop with red tin roofs and colonial style stone buildings, which were almost 150 years old, the school looked like a cozily perched building in a beautiful landscape painting. Students lived in huge dormitories which had fireplaces (though they didn't work anymore, but probably did 150 years ago when the school was filled with kids of officers from the British army). In fact, the very founder of her school was a British military officer who had died during the revolt of 1857. When Tiana was new to this school, she had no idea that it had once been a strict military school. Being put right in the middle of a life which was ruled by sounds of the bell, shrill whistles and bellowing voices of orders from day to night was not exactly what Tiana was expecting for herself! Everything was compulsory and guided by a strict set of rules and regulations . . . this meant anything from wake-up calls to strict classes and even games and hobbies (Ya! You read it right . . . even hobbies, which under normal circumstances are usually the outcome of your wishes, were compulsory here!).

Though all this was a little difficult to digest in the beginning, she slowly got used to it and then started loving it. She was genuinely grateful to her parents for sending her to such an amazing school. However, loving it did not guarantee an easy ride for anybody living there. Things were quite different within the beautiful walls of that picturesque landscape. Within a single month of living with her new classmates, she found groups and gangs sprouting like mushrooms around her. The so called 'cool gang' had formed quite visibly, right under their noses. The worst part was . . . she didn't find herself anywhere near to even getting close to that gang.

So who or what defined cool and popular anyway? She had no clue. She had not expected all this to happen and before she could say Jack-Robins, she realised that she was being left out.

She hadn't cared about it so much until the day she had an argument with one of those popular girls. The girl refused to return Tiana's book. The entire gang fought with Tiana over such a dumb thing. Not surprisingly, the rest of the class joined the militant army and automatically took their side. Tiana, of course, was relegated into the corner of the lonely. The weeks that followed were definitely some of the most miserable ones of her life.

Ever been in that dark spot where people look right through you and you are ignored to the extent that you start feeling non-existent? Well, Tiana found herself just there! Horrible things were done to her. Someone shook her cupboard and things like oil and shampoo spilled on her clothes, books and all of her important and necessary possessions. The girls joked about her and made fun of her in front of her. They didn't stop even when they saw Tiana crying. No one spoke to her for weeks! They even accused her of stealing. Worst of all, someone threw a bathroom slipper at her in the dormitory. In short, the place was nothing less than pandemonium for her! It was as if she was not even human.

The time she spent in the classes was peaceful but going back to the dormitory was torturous. Sometimes, she even hid in the bathroom for hours so that no one would see and taunt her. This went on for almost two months till those girls found a new victim and all their negative attention turned away from Tiana. Everything went back to normal as if nothing had happened.

Tiana was grateful for the change but she could not forget the hellish time she had gone through and knew that the only way to save herself from this kind of rough treatment was to become friends with these girls. But at the same time she had also made up her mind that she was not going to become rude, insolent and cheeky like them. The funny thing was that she didn't actually try to be their friend. They had to come to her. She could not lead herself to become part of some snooty girl's posse.

As it turned out, she needn't have worried anyway because as soon as she reached high school ... whoosh! Everything changed. When you are in high school, it's all about who you're going around with, how many guys are serenading around you, what you're wearing, which party you're going to and basically being 'cool'. Girls who have a bunch of boys goggling at them and asking them out are in demand. Only a handful of girls (including the popular ones) were going through this new drama and—to her own surprise—Tiana was one of them.

Because of all this attention, she was asked to hang out with the 'cool' people. Slowly, she got accepted as their new friend. That was four years ago.

She found it very amusing that the main reason why she was accepted was due to the attention she got from boys. She was only twelve then. At that time she did not realise that in another year's time, boys would become a very important or rather a major part of her friends' conversation. She knew that she was lucky. She had what she wanted. Like her friends, she enjoyed all the attention she received. But every situation has its pros and cons.

Slowly, it dawned on Tiana that she had to be very careful about what she said to or near her friends. They were, for some unknown reason, more touchy and sensitive than the rest of the girls. They were quick to express their mocking amusement at anything they considered silly. They did not even spare their own group when it came to acting scornful and sarcastic.

As Tiana did not want to be ridiculed again, she started saying those very things which she thought would be acceptable to her friends. She stopped voicing her true opinions and instead, said what they wanted to hear. A time came when the only opinion that mattered more than anything else to her friends were Tiana's false opinions.

Finally, in grade nine, when her English teacher asked all the students in her class to speak about themselves for two minutes, she realised that she had a biiiiig problem. She could not even speak about herself for thirty seconds.

She was standing in front of the class and all she could see were about thirty pairs of gaping eyes. Her mind was doing its best to recall something of her own. It quickly tried to do a complete memory scan . . . but it all turned out to be a vain effort. 'Tabula rasa my dear friend!' was the answer that her mind gave back. So that was it . . . she just stood there . . . speechless.

'Tiana come on, tell us something about your likes and dislikes. What are your hobbies? Try. It can't be that difficult,' said her teacher with a hint of irritation in her voice.

Thinking hard, she tried to concentrate on her hobbies. She liked to listen to music. No wait . . . that is what Bella (one of her friends) liked. She liked eating pizzas but only because her best friend Leila liked to do so. She thought of a number of things but after every thought, she realised that the only reason she liked to do that is because one or the other of her friends liked to do the same. The need to fit in had made her change so much that she no longer knew her own self.

What was the whole point of having friends when you can't be yourself with them? When you have to be extremely careful about what you say to them? And when you want to crack a joke but are not sure if you should because there is a very good chance that one of them will take it very personally and will start crying or get pissed off with you?

Well, that is exactly what had happened with Tiana. So, she had been extra careful to omit her true feelings whenever she was with her friends. And now that this had become a habit, she had reached the shameful state of having no clue about herself.

The sound of the bell indicating the end of class saved her from one more painful minute of staring at the wall incredulously! Her ears were burning! If people could get a peep into her imagination, they would have seen fire around her ears! It was at that moment that she finally became conscious about the main reason behind why she could not answer questions that were as simple as the ones asked in a slam book like – favourite food, favourite brand, the teacher you liked most and blah blah blah!

She generally didn't have answers to these; at least not fixed answers. It was mostly her mother or friends who made decisions for her. It was easier that way.

With every passing minute, the thought that she didn't know about herself nagged her relentlessly. She didn't even remember when she had become so artificial. Tiana felt a sudden urge to find out more about herself.

She did not want to get overshadowed by the people around her. She had forgotten how to draw a line between truth and lies, reality and make believe . . . and so she decided to find 'it' . . . her original thoughts and opinions about everything . . . answers to the very simple questions of her life.

Sitting on her bed now, she reflected that if she had not started that quest for answers so many months ago, she would probably be lying on one of the beds of the emergency room of some hospital right now. She shuddered at the thought. Someone knocked at her door but she didn't want to talk to anyone. She felt guilty and responsible for what had happened. She could have stopped it from happening. A small voice in her head told her, 'Stop kidding yourself. They wouldn't have listened to you'. Still, she could have tried. But now it was too late.

Another knock on the door brought her out of her trance. Someone was calling her name. That someone was her elder brother Sid. She didn't respond. She wanted to forget everything. She wanted to sleep . . .

TWO

'So I will see you in the evening, okay? Reach on time. Love ya, Bye,' said Leila, cheerfully into her handset.

Tiana was smiling at her best friend. Leila was on the phone (so what's new? Her cell phone was practically stuck to her ear. It was like her life line; she can't survive without it) calling all their friends to her house so that they could pack together. Their holidays were coming to an end and they had to finish their packing by the following afternoon.

Tiana hardly took any time in packing but her friends... Oh! Her friends could go on with it for days together. Packing together before leaving for Hill View High has been their ritual for the past four years. This year, they would be in class ten.

Leila got up from her bed and walked across the room towards her dressing table where she started examining her reflection, but when she caught a glimpse of Tiana in the mirror, she turned around.

'Why are you smiling?' asked Leila.

'Nothing, it's just that I find it silly that they have to carry all their stuff to your house to pack when they can easily do it at their own place,' said Tiana.

'If you have not understood till now, you never will,' sighed Leila.

Tiana and Leila had hit it off from the very beginning. Even though they are completely different, both of them got along famously and could always count on each other. Leila was considered to be one of the hottest girls in school. Her lean body, whitish complexion, shoulder length straight black hair (always straight!) with bangs and beautiful black eyes added to her charm. Leila was loud and outgoing. Tiana was fair and pretty with a curvy figure. Tiana had an oval face with brown eyes and waist length hair. Leila had a long list of ex-boyfriends. On the other hand, Tiana had a long list of boys wanting to go out with her. But she refused to date. She felt that she was in no rush. She decided that she would date only when she genuinely liked someone.

She had seen her friends date just for the heck of it or because having a boyfriend was supposed to be very cool and socially necessary. Her friends kept on fighting with their boyfriends over the dumbest reasons ever. At the same time, they kept asking Tiana irritating questions like, 'Tiana, why didn't he ring me up this afternoon?', 'Will he like this dress?', 'What should I gift him?', 'Why did he fight with me?', 'I am getting hiccoughs, do you think he is missing me?', etc.

Hell! How was she supposed to know what they liked when she didn't even know what she liked!

But she had started working on that problem. She had not confided about this to any of her friends. By now she knew them well enough to know that they were not good at accepting new ideas. They would never understand exactly what it was that she was she trying to find. To be honest, at that time, even she didn't know how to go about it. Where to start? To combat her problem head on, she first made a rough mental list of things she was confused about. Well, at least it was a start . . .

1. My favourite movie
2. My favourite kind of food
3. My most embarrassing moment
4. My thoughts about my friends
5. My favourite actor
6. My favourite colour

7. My favourite quote
8. My greatest wish
9. And am I happy with my life?
She was planning on finding honest answers. HONEST.

'Hey, did I tell you my mom and dad are going to Paris after my holidays get over? I wish I could miss school and go with them,' moaned Leila, interrupting Tiana's interior monologue.

Leila's dad was a well known photographer. He travelled all over the world. One could never get bored when her father was around. He always had the most fascinating stories from every corner of the world. Even Tiana felt a little jealous of him this time. She had always wanted to go to Paris. This was one place that she was dying to visit since the first time she had seen the lit-up Eiffel tower in a photograph.

'Never mind Leila. Maybe you will be luckier some other time.'

'Wow, what a consolation!' muttered Leila.

It occurred to Tiana that for once she had an honest answer. She was positive that Paris was the only city she so wished to see. This was an original thought. She was still very happy about this when the rest of their friends came to Leila's house to start the packing ritual.

∽

'What time are the guys coming to pick us up?' asked Bella.

'I don't know, Tiana spoke to them,' added Lilly.

Bella looked at Tiana. Tiana was fuming. For the past one hour Bella, Celia, Savera, Lilly, Aliya and Leila had been talking about nothing but their boyfriends (that is, except for Lilly, who did not have a boyfriend but was talking about boys in general). The bottom line was that their inane conversation dragged on and on and on about the same old topic – boys.

Since the time they had started dating, all they cared about were their boyfriends. But that was not what irritated her the most. What was making her angrier by the minute was what she had just discovered. While talking about their boyfriends, they had let slip something they had been hiding from Tiana.

It was the fact that the boys had a new name for Tiana. These days they were referring to her as Ice Princess. This re-christening was supposedly because they thought that she had no feelings as she kept refusing to go out with any guy. As if!!!

The fact that the boys called her this was not what hurt her. They came up with a new nickname for anybody and everybody every month. What really hurt Tiana was that her friends knew about this new nickname and still had not breathed a word about it to her. They had been taking their boyfriends' side! How atrocious! Now for the past half-an-hour, she had been sitting quietly on Leila's bean bag in the corner of the room, thinking about this. She had finished her packing way before the rest. The rest were not even half way through.

Bella was still looking at her. Did Bella seriously expect Tiana to answer a question referring to boys? Those scumbags? It was no wonder that so many girls had just started going out, not because they wanted to, but because idiotic people started to make fun of them if they did not do so. This is the most ridiculous part of a teenager's life – sometimes you just have to do things because the others do it and it is considered to be 'oh so cool'. And the boys could not bear the thought of any girl ignoring them for long. Tiana had done so, and that is why they had given her a cruel nickname to settle scores. The cheek that those ego-maniacs had!

She knew that even if the entire world made fun of her she would not do something she didn't believe in. She just wished that the other girls would also get the courage to be like her and not tumble under the so called 'peer pressure'. How dare someone else manipulate her decisions! Tiana rolled her eyes heavenwards in exasperation.

By the time her eyes reached earth level, she suddenly realised that she hadn't entirely lost her individuality. Her lips slowly twitched into a smile as she thought about this. She still was very close to her real thoughts; it just needed some working on. And if her real thoughts were like the way she felt now, then discovering the rest of them was surely going to be a lot of fun.

'Why are you smiling Tia?' quizzed Leila.

She looked up and was tempted to tell all of them about her 'finding it' theory but decided that now was not the right time to do so.

'Nothing important. I am going to get something to eat,' replied Tiana.

She got up from the bean bag to go to the kitchen. As she closed the door behind her, she heard Savera say, 'Tia is acting a little weird'.

Tiana smiled to herself again. Her friends were getting confused. Good, she thought as she entered the kitchen.

Karam, Leila's elder brother, was sitting at the breakfast counter. He had just made himself an enormous sandwich.

'So how is the packing going on?' grinned Karam.

'Very very slow. Only I am through,' replied Tiana, taking out an apple from the fridge and joining him at the counter.

He laughed. Karam was a year older than Leila. He too found the packing ritual ridiculous.

'So this year, all of you are going to class ten. Best of luck! Every teacher will be giving you a lengthy lecture about the Boards,' said Karam.

'Thank you for reminding me, but this topic is much better than the one being discussed upstairs in your sister's room,' replied Tiana.

'What can be worse than the Boards?' he asked.

'That's easy. Boys,' quipped Tiana.

'We feel the same way about you girls,' laughed Karam.

'I am sure. I am sure. No wonder I am being called Ice Princess currently.' Her voice was bitter with anger.

Karam sensed that and said, 'Oh! So that nickname has finally reached your ears. See, you just have to ignore them.'

'And even you knew about it?' questioned Tiana, her eyebrows rising into a high arch.

'Yes, I did,' but seeing the look on her face he added, 'How could I have told you about it when it was something that even your best friend was not willing to reveal?'

'Yeah, I guess you have a point there,' sighed Tiana.

'Leila told me that all of you are going out tonight,' said Karam, trying to change the subject.

'Not just us. Even you are coming with us. Without you I won't be able to control them. You know that!' said Tiana.

'Yeah, but my sister does not want her elder brother around. She has not even asked me to come,' said Karam knowingly.

'Okay. Firstly, she is not that little. You are just a year older than us. And secondly, it is not her plan. It is Rehan's plan and he would want you to come. So you are coming. Otherwise, how will I transport them back to their houses?' asked Tiana.

Karam laughed at that. He understood what Tiana meant. For quite a while now, Tiana's friends had begun to drink at social gatherings. They were usually drunk by the end of the party and as Tiana, Sid and Karam were the only non-drinkers, the fate of delivering all of them in one piece to their houses fell on their shoulders. It was not an easy task to support them . . . especially when they were puking.

'Gosh! What is that smell?' snorted Tiana when she entered the room again.

Instead of answering her, her friends gathered around her and very firmly asked her to sit down. She had a faint idea about what was going on in their mind but she didn't say anything. She wanted to be sure before she made any kind of statement.

'Look T, all of us are sorry that we hid your nick name from you. Please, can we forget about it now?' said Bella cajolingly.

Easy for her to say! Tiana tightened her lips but managed to say casually, 'Sure it is alright, but if something like this happens again, do let me know.'

'Yes, we promise that but we also feel that you have been acting a little weird,' said Savera.

'And I agree with Savera,' said Celia.

Everyone agreed with Savera. She was always supposed to be right (and generally, she was!). To describe Savera, the only word which comes to my mind is PROPER. She is perfect in almost every way. She is tall and fair with long curly hair and dark round eyes. Everyone likes her for a lot of reasons like –

- She is a brain (and the only one who has spectacles on). Therefore, the teachers love her.
- She speaks what's on her mind honestly so there is no need or occasion for bitching.
- She's a problem solver.
- And finally, she never gets into trouble.

Her boyfriend Aryan is decent too. However, they cannot resist fighting and arguing with each other either! But their fights were not over silly reasons. They don't act childish and were unlike the rest of her friends.

All of them were looking at Tiana expecting an answer that would explain her weird behaviour. Maybe she should tell them. She would have to do so sooner or later anyway. Why not sooner?

She took a deep breath and began choosing her words carefully, 'Okay, if you want the truth then listen carefully. Recently, I have realised that since the time I became friends with you guys, I have just constantly been trying to fit in with you people. Through the years, I have changed a lot. I have lost my own identity in trying to mould myself to what you like and what you want me to be.' Leila opened her mouth to protest but Tiana raised her hand and stopped her. The rest of her friends were staring at her as if she had gone bonkers. 'It is not at all your fault,' Tiana continued, 'it is entirely my mistake. And so I have decided to get back in touch with my real, true and original ideas, thoughts and opinions. And that's the main reason why I kind of seem lost when all of us are talking about something particular. It is because I start thinking about what I genuinely feel. That's the truth for you. I am trying to find answers,' finished Tiana and then studied her friends' bewildered faces. They looked completely zapped.

Her lips were twitching vigourously, dying to spread out into a smile. However, she controlled that nearly uncontrollable desire by pressing her lips tightly together. All of them were staring at her blankly. Bella recovered before the rest of them.

'That is the dumbest thing I have ever heard. Tiana, don't act so weird.'

Tiana personally felt that by now, Bella should be used to hearing dumb stuff, considering the fact that she was dating Veer, the dumbest boy in school.

Bella happened to be the most attractive girl in school after Leila. She is pretty, cute (thanks to her dimples), has a petite figure, neck length hair (streaked brown) and big beautiful eyes. She is smart, intelligent and has a great sense of fashion but still, she was dating a guy who had never passed in any subject, in his entire life, without reappearing for it at least once. He ate with his mouth open, and talked with chunks of food in his mouth . . . happily displaying the gross scene to all the unfortunate ones on earth. As for his clothes, they could have done with some regular and vigourous washing.

'I knew that you would not understand, and that is exactly why I did not want to tell you. But now you know about it. Please do not joke about it because this is important to me, okay?' pleaded Tiana.

'Hey, we won't tease you about it. Relax, okay? Just tell me what time are the guys coming to pick us up?' asked Bella, carelessly changing the subject.

'Is that all you care about?' asked Tiana in a oh-no-not-again manner.

'Care about what?' Bella questioned, wide eyed.

'Boys,' replied Tiana. Bella looked at her as if Tiana was losing her nut.

'I mean, you spend most part of the day with them and you talk about them even in the little bit of time that we get to spend together. Don't you get sick of it? Don't you get bored?' asked Tiana.

It was so true. Since her friends had started dating, they hardly ever hung out together as they used to. Something had changed. During the holidays, they spent most of their time with their boyfriends. At school, the only time Tiana saw them all together was in the dormitories at night . . . and that too because the dorms were locked at night. Otherwise, she was pretty sure that they would have dated during the night too. She missed her friends.

Now that Tiana was in the 'finding it' mode, she didn't care much if they thought that she was different. Here she was, putting in her heart and soul in trying to 'find it', and her friends? Just look at them. They had changed themselves according to their boyfriends' whims and fancies.

Leila started speaking slowly, 'Tiana, how can we get bored with guys? They are not a punishment for us. We like them. They have become a very important part of our lives.' It was as if Tiana was suddenly growing deaf and she needed to be explained things carefully.

Tiana mentally pursed her lips. There you go again! It was as if she had been banging her head against a wall. Now what could she say to make them understand her point?

'And that is why I think you should start dating,' said Leila, pouncing on Tiana.

'Not again! Don't start that again Leila,' moaned Tiana.

For as long as Tiana could remember, Leila had been trying to set her up with a guy without success. Just because she is happy with her boyfriend, she thought that having one is the best thing that can happen to a girl. Leila's boyfriend was perfect in every way. He was always there to help her. He gave her lovely gifts. He never said rude things to her or argued with her. He was very good-looking too. In fact, there was nothing that could cause a rift between them, and that was exactly what caused Tiana to fume. It wasn't as if she was jealous. Oh no! Absolutely not! It angered her because Leila's boyfriend happened to be Tiana's elder brother, Siddharth. Talk about invasion of privacy! Her PRIVACY!

Which normal girl would want her best friend to date her elder brother? This meant that she had to watch her very irritating and nosy brother join the gang whenever they got together. It also meant that she had to watch him sit there, holding Leila's hand or hugging her and whispering and giggling away or ewwww! Whatever! Who wants an extra and irritating family member around?

Family and friends were different parts of her life and now, thanks to her brother they were getting merged together to make a dangerous and unwanted alloy for Tiana. The worst part of all this was that her brother had been sharing everything the gang did with her father and cousin brothers . . . which meant that they had a fabulous time teasing her about the doings of the gang. Those were the times when she wanted to know about what kind of sin she had committed in her past life to be given the gift of so many irritating brothers in this one.

But in a way, she was the cause of her own embarrassment. Almost a year ago, she had made the mistake of giving a dare to Leila. Leila loved to play Truth and Dare, and she enjoyed giving everybody around her amazingly wacky dares. Tiana had received a significant amount of tiresome dares from her and this time, she got a chance to give Leila a dose of her own medicine. She dared Leila to make her brother Sid date some cool girl within ten days.

Tiana knew that her brother was not interested in dating and was busy with his first love – music. According to her, she was giving Leila a dare that would be synonymous with 'impossible'. She spent quite a few moments basking in the glory of her anticipated victory. Unfortunately for her, she had to swallow the bitter pill of realising how wrong she was! Trust Leila to do anything. Within a week, Sid and Leila were not only dating but were really falling head over heels for each other. On the one hand, it was amazing, and on the other hand, it was so ewwww!

She had asked Leila to make him date some girl, not her! What the ?!*?#!%? But, on reminding Leila about this fact, she replied coolly, 'Hey, you said some girl . . . not which girl. So, I can be some girl too.'

Of course, it was logical, and that's it. End of topic.

And now, her elder brother and best friend have been dating for more than a year.

'Tiana, this time I really mean it. You just have to say yes to the next guy who will ask you out, okay?' said Leila with a strong hint of a threat in her tone.

Leila's voice brought Tiana back to reality. She glared back at her best friend with a 'oh yeah, says who?' look.

'What is this, a threat? And no, I will not say yes to any random guy, okay. Drop it,' said Tiana even more firmly.

Leila snorted. She thought of Tiana as her ultimate challenge. As far as Leila is concerned, she was the perfect matchmaker. She could make anyone date anyone. But as far as Tiana is concerned, hmmmmm, no such luck. No wonder Leila often sounded rather desperate. She really wanted everybody to be as happy as she was, and Tiana's case was the only black spot in her long list of successful match-makings.

'If you are planning on drilling me about this useless topic, then you can enjoy by yourself tonight because I refuse to come,' said Tiana.

'Don't be such a spoilt sport T. You have to come, okay?' said Aliya, signaling Leila to back down. Aliya knew that Tiana was not much of a party person, and she would take the help of any excuse to back out of any kind of socialising. Aliya is good with this sort of stuff. She is the sensitive kind. Most of the time, it's because of Aliya that they don't end up fighting. Aliya is short (compared to the rest of them) and very fair, with a heart shaped face and small beady eyes. She has a slight accent because she had lived in the USA for a few years.

The end of holidays fever was riding high on everybody. Tiana knew that everybody would get pissed off if she did not go with them and that is why she had reluctantly agreed to go. If she found any excuse to wriggle out, she would take it in a jiffy, and that included Leila's non-stop pestering.

'Tiana, for the last time without getting angry or without giving us an absurd answer, please tell me when will the guys come to pick us up?' asked Bella for the third time. Tiana smiled at her.

'I am sorry. I owe you that answer. I spoke to Veer and he said that Aryan and Zain will come to pick us up at eight. We will meet the rest of them at Electric,' said Tiana. Electric was the new joint that Rehan's dad had opened quite recently. It was on number one position in the latest list of cool hang-out places. Electric was the flavour of the month for the teenage tribe.

'Thank you. Now I can dress accordingly,' said Bella gratefully 'Maybe I should wear the new dress daddy got for me.'

On many occasions just like this one, Bella reminded Tiana of Veronica Lodge from the gang in Archies comics. Maybe it was the way she called her father 'daddy' (Tiana nearly expected her to say daddikins sometimes!) or acted poor little rich daddy's girl on purpose or naturally. The similarity was uncanny, especially when Bella acted like a fashion freak, which was oh-so-often. Tiana decided that maybe someday she would tell her this.

At ten to eight, Aryan and (to Tiana's utmost disappointment) Sid came to pick them up.

'What are you doing here?' groaned Tiana, already sure that she was not going to enjoy herself tonight.

'What do you mean Tiana? Rehan invited me, so what's your problem? Look, I don't want to fight with you tonight, okay. I just want to be with Leila,' he shot back.

So now, it was official – she will not be seeing much of her best friend tonight. *C'est merveilleux! Très fantastique**, she did not think.

'I don't want to fight with you either,' said Tiana for her friends' sake. Leila threw Tiana a thankful look. She didn't want to spoil any one else's night even though hers was undoubtedly going down the drain. When they reached the club, Zain, Rehan, Veer and Karam were waiting for them outside. While going inside, Tiana asked Karam, 'So, you made it huh?'

'Well, it's my greatest ambition to get puked on and I couldn't have left this important job for Sid and you,' grinned Karam.

'Thank you for wanting to share the glorious feeling,' she grinned back.

Electric really had an electrifying ambience that never failed to captivate. Unlike the other clubs where getting space for one tiny foot was considered to be a task, this club was very spacious. With its colour scheme of thrilling blue and white, contemporary looks and plush interiors, it promised to be a lot of fun. It had round tables scattered around the dance floor and the DJ was playing groovy tracks. Surprisingly, no one was dancing.

All of them sat around a huge round table. Tiana liked being in this place. Being big and spacious, it was not like the other places which constantly smelled of smoke, floor polish and sweat. Yukh! She always felt claustrophobic in such places. Everyone was ordering their drinks and when she was asked what she wanted, she replied, 'A coke please, thank you.'

'Okay guys, today I dare Tiana to drink a real drink. What say everyone?' said Veer loudly, sarcasm reeling under his horrid voice.

Tiana gave him the dirtiest look she could muster. She had had enough! Veer was the jerk who had named her Ice Princess. And she knew why.

---

*That's marvellous! Very fantastic!

She had hurt his pathetic ego by refusing to go out with him when he had asked her out six months ago. A day after she had refused to go out with him, he had come up to her and slapped her! Her friends believe he did this because Tiana had embarrassed him and he wanted to show his one-upmanship by embarrassing her. If that was the case, then his plan had backfired because Tiana had slapped him (and hard!) back right in front of all her friends.

She knew that now all he wanted to do was to make things difficult for her. But she was not the weakling that he thought she was. She was not going to buckle under his pressure. If anything, she was going to make things difficult for him. Besides, she was angry with each and every guy sitting at the table and wanted to give them an earful for this entire Ice Princess nonsense. So, she braced herself for what was going to happen.

'What part of your chauvinist brain thinks that coke is not a real drink?' she growled.

'Chauv what? Nah! You are just a chicken! You're afraid of the dare,' came the reply from the bird brain.

'CHAUVINIST! And it will take more than that to break an ice princess, don't you think?' Tiana said mockingly.

'Well you ARE an ice princess. Don't blame the name I've given you,' said Veer.

'I thought that was my name,' said Tiana.

'What?'

'So now you are an ice princess, is that so?' said Tiana.

'No, you are,' said he, baffled with what had just happened.

But she had been successful in what she had wanted to do. Veer is no doubt the dumbest guy in school. She easily confused him with his own words. But now that she had her chance, she wanted to go on.

'So you still want to give me stupid dares, Veer? You feel that you are so mature and manly sitting over there, drinking vodka and polluting the atmosphere with your cancer sticks? Go on, go on, be my guest, sipping poison with so much relish. You are just conning yourself to feel that you are macho, stylish and cool. When you realise this, it will be too late. So don't you dare try and put me in your league. I can't stop you but I suggest you learn how to behave around me because I don't know about the rest of them,' Tiana waved a careless hand towards the gang, 'but I will not take any kind of crap from you in future, you moron!' finished Tiana, feeling considerably lighter and happier.

'But that does not change anything,' said Rehan.

'What was supposed to change?' asked Tiana, turning to look at Rehan.

'I mean, you are still an ice princess whether you like it or not. You refuse every guy who tries to ask you out without a proper reason. I mean, either you are icy or you are just not attracted . . . to boys,' finished Rehan, a little hesitantly.

She couldn't believe what she was hearing! So that is what these brain dead guys think about her. That was going to be her next nick name! She looked around the table. Clearly, all her friends and Sid and Karam were as surprised to hear this as she was. Tiana now looked positively militant.

'Oh! My God, this is the limit! So that is what you guys think about me, huh? Amazing! Firstly, just because I don't give you a reason behind each and every decision of mine, it does not mean that the reason doesn't exist! You guys need to set your priorities right! Maybe you have forgotten. Let me remind you about what you all called me two years ago when according to some of you, (she looked at Aryan and Veer with a sneer, as they uncomfortably shifted in their chairs and tried to avoid her glare) I was becoming overfriendly with the boys of our class. Right now when I am not so friendly with boys, I have become a lesbian, and when I was friendly with guys, then I was a slut! Bloody hell! Who do you think you are? Think about that now!' roared Tiana, as her justifiable anger levels and voice levels reached maximum point, forgetting that she was in a public place.

The room was suddenly quiet and everyone was staring at her, astonished at her unrestrained language. The guys at her table, she was pleased to notice, looked confused and embarrassed. Serves them right! Seething with rage, she got up from the table and said menacingly, 'Excuse me, I need to to go to the wash room,' and with that she walked across the room, conscious that every eye in the room was following her. Once inside the ladies room, she gained her composure again. She now found the entire thing hilarious. She rarely lost her temper but today was just one of those days. Bad luck for those guys. It was in their kismet to be the victims of her fury.

She was laughing when Leila, Bella and Savera came in to check on her.

'Now I am positive that she has lost her mind. Look at her! She is laughing and I thought she would be angry,' said Bella with a weak smile. 'Tiana, I am really sorry about what Veer did and said outside,' she said in a serious tone.

'Don't be silly. He should be sorry, not you. And just to make things clear, I am not attracted to any of you, okay? That would be gross and eeegggh!' replied Tiana, shuddering a little dramatically. All of them laughed.

'Don't be silly T. We know that. I was so shocked to hear Rehan say that! Don't mind them, they are already feeling sorry,' said Leila.

'I wonder how you managed to make them feel guilty so easily. I can never make Veer feel guilty and sorry when he fights with me. I must learn the knack from you,' laughed Bella.

'You never lose your temper Tia. I think your shouting and biting answers shocked them,' said Savera.

'I hope you are alright,' said Leila.

'Are you kidding me? I am feeling great after all the shouting and telling them what the score is. I am sorry, but I think your boyfriends deserved it,' replied Tiana.

'Oh yes! I completely agree. They acted like ultimate losers tonight. What did you call them before leaving the table?' asked Bella.

'Morons,' muttered Tiana half smiling. 'For the first time, you are not taking their side,' said Tiana, feeling really victorious. This was actually an achievement!

'That's because till now, we didn't know that they are morons,' replied Leila giving an apologetic smile to Tiana.

Five minutes later when she sat down at the table again, she was feeling much better. None of the boys had the guts to say anything lest Tiana started yelling again. But Rehan tried, 'Look Tiana, we are . . .'

'I don't care,' she cut him off. Sensing that he was going to say something else, she looked at him squarely in the eye and said matter-of-factly, 'And I don't want to talk about it.' That shut his mouth.

After a minute of uncomfortable silence during which no one was looking at Tiana, Sid spoke up.

'I did not know that my little sister could get so angry.'

The talk-to-me-at-your-own-risk look that she gave him shut him up too.

'Sid, I don't want to talk about what just happened,' she reminded him.

'So lets talk about some thing else then. We can't sit in silence for the rest of the night now, can we?' he said, trying to lighten up things.

'Alright. Like what?' asked Leila.

Tiana decided to test their endurance level. As it was, her friends were seeing her new side (thanks to the 'finding it' theory) . . . a bit more would not hurt. She wanted to step up her research to a higher level anyway.

'Okay then, there is something I have been wanting to ask all of you. May I?' she asked frankly to no one in particular.

'Sure,' said Aryan.

'Do you have a favourite movie?' asked Tiana, looking at him.

Everyone looked at her in amazement. She smiled to herself. Must be odd for them to first see her shouting angrily and then in a matter of few minutes, begin to discuss movies so calmly. Aryan looked very confused.

'Is this a trick question? I mean, you won't make fun of me if I answer that, will you?' asked Aryan suspiciously.

'No I will do no such thing, don't worry,' replied Tiana, amused by his question. No doubt she had made a new impression on these guys.

And now, they will either respect her or be more careful around her. Suits her!

'My favourite movie is *The Matrix,*' replied Aryan, more confidently.

'Why is that your favourite movie?' asked Tiana as soon as he finished speaking.

Taken aback, he replied, 'I haven't really thought about why. I guess it's because I find the action sequences pretty cool. Is that good enough?' he asked.

'Yes, good enough. Anyone else who wants to answer my question?' Tiana looked at the rest of them.

'Yes, I want to. My favourite movie is *A Cinderella Story,*' said Bella.

'Why Bella, why?' asked Tiana.

'Because I like Hilary Duff and Chad Michael Murray is hot,' exclaimed Bella.

'Hello? Remember I am your boyfriend,' said Veer in disbelief.

Both Bella and Tiana ignored him.

'That's it. No other reason? You like the movie because Chad is hot?' asked Tiana.

'Yes, it is very simple, you either like something or you don't. That's the only reason which comes into my mind,' replied Bella simply. Good enough again, thought Tiana. She looked at the rest of her friends questioningly.

'My favourite movie is *Mean Girls* because it is so funny and true,' said Leila.

'Mine is *Pirates of the Caribbean* and I don't know why. It just is,' said Savera.

'There must be some reason,' prodded Tiana.

'Actually, it's not important to have a reason behind everything,' said Veer, a little cautiously because the last time he had spoken to Tiana, she had acted like a tigress. 'My favourite movie is *Superman*, and all its sequels too. It's because I like Superman. It is as simple as that,' he finished, probably making the first sensible statement in his life. So Veer was not so dumb. 'What about you?' he asked Tiana.

She kept quiet and took her time before saying anything. But Leila exclaimed, 'Wait a minute, does this have anything to do with your finding it quest?' Leila was very sharp.

'Yes it does have something to do with it. I just wanted to know about your favourite things and why they were your favourite,' replied Tiana.

All the guys looked very confused. So Savera explained the situation to them.

'So which is your favourite movie and why?' Veer repeated.

'I have been trying to think about that for some time now. I just . . . don't know!' Tiana said with a helpless look about her.

'Don't sweat it T. Let us help you. I will ask you some questions. In fact, all of us will ask you questions. You just have to give us your instinctive answers. Are you willing to try that?' asked Sid.

Great, she was just about to give everyone at the table a right to ask her any question.

'Sure, if it will help,' sighed Tiana.

'Great! Do you like action flicks?' asked Sid.

'No.'

'What about comedies?' joined in Bella.

'Romantic comedies, yes, I like them,' replied Tiana truthfully.

'Who is your favourite actress?' asked Karam.

'How will that help?'

'Oh! You never know! Think and tell us,' said Leila.

Her favourite actress. Hmm, that was one of the questions from her list! And the answer came so suddenly and easily. Maybe it was because she already knew the answer to this question.

'I like Audrey Hepburn for her elegance, grace and style. Also she was beautiful, especially her eyes,' said Tiana.

'That was quick,' said Leila.

'I know but I guess I already knew this one,' said Tiana.

'Wait a minute, who is Audrey Hepburn?' asked Rehan.

'Rehan, just forget it okay,' said Celia, a bit exasperated with her boyfriend.

'Audrey Hepburn, hmm . . . that means you like impeccably dressed people around you and in the movies you watch,' stated Bella.

What did Bella say? Impeccably dressed people. Was that true?

'Bella, you make me sound so snobbish and arrogant,' said Tiana.

'Yes Bella, what makes you think that? I mean, that's dumb!' quipped Aliya.

'Tiana, it's an honest observation. You do so, you do! There is nothing snobbish, or different or arrogant about wanting to be surrounded by well-dressed people,' said Bella.

Tiana thought about it and realised that it was true. She couldn't believe that of all people, it was Bella who had realised this, but it was so true. Wow! Come to think of it, she had always wanted to go to Paris, the fashion capital of the world. And she would love to work in a fashion magazine . . . maybe even become its editor someday. Oh God! That was so true! Tiana was amazed to discover this new aspect of her personality. She was so excited that she didn't even hear what Karam was saying to her. She had to ask him to repeat what he said.

'See, my question helped. And clearly, you seem very happy about it,' said Karam. She smiled at him and nodded her grateful thanks.

'We still don't know about your favourite movie though,' reminded Leila.

'Okay, let's solve the mystery then,' said Sid, and counting on his fingers he started, 'You like romantic comedies. You like impeccably dressed people (he winked at Bella) according to Bella. I already know that you love Paris and that you would love to work in a fashion magazine. Tiana, do you remember seeing any movie with anything or maybe everything from this list? Try and think,' nudged Sid.

A movie with Paris, a chic magazine and lots of beautiful clothes. Of course! She knew which one was her favourite movie right then.

'I know!' sang out Tiana happily.

Everyone was looking at her in expectation.

'So will you please tell us? I am dying of suspense here. After all, we have helped you in your quest. Hurry up T, tell us,' said Bella urgently. Tiana smiled at Bella's enthusiasm.

'The Devil Wears Prada,' said Tiana excitedly.

'Oh! Perfect choice Tia,' said Leila and as though counting the list in her head, she added, 'and it has everything that you like!' she concluded happily.

'I know! Thanks you guys. It feels so good. I now have the answer for two questions on my list,' said Tiana gratefully. This had been easy. And Sid of all the people had helped her.

'Wait, what was the name of the movie again?' asked Veer, squinting his eyes in an attempt to remember the name.

'The Devil Wears Prada,' replied Bella.

'Is that even a movie? I have never heard of it,' said Veer mockingly.

'Nor have I,' said Rehan.

'Me neither,' added Aryan vaguely, wriggling his hand and looking at the ceiling.

Tiana's temper had begun to rise again. These boys would never change. So, might as well handle them like they deserved to be handled . . . like intellectually negligible creatures.

'That's the difference between you and me,' said Tiana in an icy cool voice, which was the opposite of what she was feeling inside.

'You boys live in the world of fantasy, of Superman and the Matrix. Nothing is wrong with that. I love Superman too. But the difference is that I, unlike you, also know that other things exist and I, unlike you again, am actually able to like those other things. So unless you want to have another argument with me and believe me, I will win again, you guys had better stitch your mouths,' finished Tiana in the same cool voice. It did the trick and shut their traps.

'Tiana, I am seeing a totally new you tonight. What's up? You were never like this sis,' asked a bewildered Sid.

'On the contrary bro, I have always been like this. Only till now I was doing all the listening. I have been listening to gits like Veer pass comments on me as if I were made of stone. But that's it. I have been too busy pleasing everyone. I have realised that no matter what I do, I can never keep everyone happy. So now, I will do the talking and tonight was just a preview,' said Tiana. Sid looked at her as if he was seeing her for the first time.

'Actually, to be honest, I have seen you fight like this once before with the girls who were my classmates last year,' said Sid.

'Oh yeah! I completely forgot about that fight!' exclaimed Leila.

'How could you forget? That fight was classic!' said Bella.

Tiana had to agree. That was a really big fight. Tiana and her friends were in class nine last year while Sid's classmates were in class twelve. Just because they were seniors, they thought that they had the right to give a hard time to the juniors. Their list of whims and fancies that were to be fulfilled by the juniors included bullying them into doing favours of all kinds. These could range from bringing water early in the morning to washing their clothes at twelve in the night. And even though bringing water is not such a big deal but hey! Come on, Tiana was not going to let herself be some snooty senior's personal maid! Besides, were 'the seniors' really so lazy?

Tiana knew that this bullying and favours thing was an unofficial school rule. The moment girls or boys would reach class twelve, they would just assume that it was their birthright to make the juniors' lives miserable. Teachers don't help much. It's also important for teachers to be on good terms with the class twelve girls as they are prefects and control the students for teachers.

But just because nobody had had the guts to speak out for so many years didn't mean that Tiana had to keep taking this nonsense. She decided to rebel against the seniors. So if any senior asked her to bring water, find stamps, wash clothes or get food, she refused point blank! Obviously seniors were shocked at first and they just said dumb stuff like 'you've had it' or 'watch out' or 'see me in the dorms'. But the truth is that seniors can't do anything. They couldn't touch Tiana because she would not tolerate that and they couldn't give her drills because she had not done anything wrong. What other authority do they have? As a result, favours reduced a lot for the rest of her batch-mates and completely stopped for Tiana.

At first, her friends were very scared and completely against this idea. They told her that it's okay and that it's an experience . . . a part of growing up in a boarding school. Tiana didn't think so. It doesn't have to be 'an experience' if you don't want it to be. And Tiana didn't want experience which was a synonym to being a servant. So, she did what she had to do. Looking back, there is nothing that she would have done differently.

'You guys better be careful around my sister in future . . . that is, if you don't want your heads bitten off,' joked Sid.

'They needn't worry about that, I don't eat hair,' replied Tiana dryly.

'You know what? Tonight has not been the way I had thought it would be. I mean all this arguing and stuff. Not fun at all,' said Leila.

'That's right. It kind of sucked tonight,' added Lilly.

'I want to go home,' said Tiana.

'Me too,' yawned Leila.

'Hey we want to stay. Please guys,' pleaded Bella and Savera.

'I can take Leila and Tiana home,' offered Karam.

'Thanks brother,' said Leila, 'Get up Tia. Let's go.'

THREE

Next morning, Sid's voice woke her up. He was in her room. In her room! He was never welcome in her room.

'What the hell are you doing here?' she cried indignantly.

'Tiana, my album's release date has been fixed! In exactly two months, your bro is going to be a rock star! And all of you will be here on a week's break from school at that time. Isn't it cool? All of you will be with me at my launch party,' said Sid, glowing with his new-found glory.

And with that, he came and gave her a big brother type goofy hug. Tiana was really happy for him. Sid was an excellent guitarist and singer and finally, his dream was coming true. His album had been recorded and now, it would be released soon.

'Congratulations Sid! I am so happy for you. I wouldn't have missed your big night for anything,' she replied, equally excited.

It was true, she meant it. No matter how irritating and bugging he may be, she loved her brother. After all, he was both family and friend.

'And thanks for helping me figure out my answer last night,' said Tiana.

'You are welcome. Now I have to go and tell Leila about this. See you later.' Saying this, Sid charged out of her room.

Half-an-hour later, she went downstairs to the dining room. Her mom was sitting there finishing the last crumbs of her breakfast. Tiana's mom was her inspiration. She did a wonderful job of being a full-time mom and career woman. Tiana loved to spend time with her and was very close to her mother. Her friends did not understand this emotional bond because they themselves did not get along too well with their own mothers and were constantly arguing with them.

'Good morning mom!' said Tiana, kissing her mom on the forehead.

'Morning honey! You heard about your brother's big news, didn't you?' smiled her mom.

'Yes, I did. He came shouting into my bedroom.'

'Sid told me about what happened last night. I think it's great that you are finally standing up for yourself. And this "finding it" business sounds like fun. I hope you achieve what you want to honey.'

'Thanks mom! You know, you are the only one who has been totally supportive about this till now. It means a lot to me,' said Tiana, touched by the fact that at least her mom understood her.

'I will always be there for you. And by the way, *The Devil Wears Prada* is my favourite too. Now I have to rush,' said her mom, while getting up and heading for the door. 'Please take care of the packing and have a good day, love you!'

Tiana's cell phone rang just as her mother left the room. It was Leila.

'Hi, what's happening?' asked Tiana.

'You need to come over here quickly Tia,' said Leila urgently.

'Why, what's wrong?'

'Please just come, okay,' and she hung the phone. Leila was being very mysterious. Strange. But she got ready quickly and left for Leila's house. When she entered Leila's room, it was jam-packed. Everyone was there—Bella, Veer, Savera, Aryan, Leila, Sid, Celia, Rehan, Aliya, Zain, Lilly and Karam.

'Okay, so what is going on? That phone call sounded like an emergency call,' said Tiana, taken aback by the number of people staring at her in the room.

'We convinced the guys that the way they behaved with you was pathetic. And they are sorry about last night. They want to apologise,' explained Bella.

Tiana could make out from the guys' faces that they were anything but sorry, and were just dying to get out of the room.

'You didn't have to do all this. They don't have to say sorry if they don't want to. It is alright. I already know that they will remain jerks forever,' said Tiana.

'Look we are really sorry. You were correct. We guys can be atrociously rude and we agree that we need to set our priorities right,' said Aryan. He held out his hand and said, 'Truce?'

'Truce.' She shook his hand. Getting them to say this much itself seemed like a herculean task. If she started hoping for them to really feel sorry . . . well, she might as well aim for the stars.

'Okay then, now that my friend is not at war with my boyfriend, let's go get something to eat. I am starving,' said Bella cheerfully.

They went outside where the cars were parked when Tiana realised that she had left her bag inside.

'I forgot my bag. I'll just go get it,' said Tiana, and rushed back into the house.

When she entered, she saw Veer walking down the stairs with her bag in his hand.

'I think you forgot this in the room,' said he.

'Yes, thank you,' replied Tiana, taking the bag from him. He didn't let go.

'I am sorry about last night. I didn't mean to make you angry,' said Veer.

'Well, you did make me angry but it's okay. Can you please let go of my bag Veer?' said Tiana, feeling queasy about the whole situation.

'I just wanted you to talk to me,' he continued, 'I still like you . . . a lot. Please go out with me Tiana.'

She looked at him in disbelief! Holy cow! Was he out of his crazy mind?

'You are going out with one of my best friends! How dare you talk to me like that, you sick pervert! Get out of my way!' shouted Tiana.

She rushed outside. She couldn't believe what had just happened. The nerve of that . . . asshole!

Outside everyone was waiting for her.

'What took you so long,' asked Bella. How could she tell Bella that she was dating a jerk?

'Nothing, I couldn't find it,' muttered Tiana.

'Oh! And was Veer inside? I don't know where he is,' asked Bella.

'Here I am. I was in the washroom,' said Veer. He was trying to act as if nothing had happened, but he avoided looking in Tiana's direction.

This is what happens when the guys you refuse to date end up dating your best friends, thought Tiana bitterly. Almost all the guys who were dating her friends had asked her out before (Veer, Aryan, and Rehan). But of course, she refused to date them. And now that this was happening, it would make life difficult for any girl because of these reasons:-

- Whenever you have a fight with one of your friends, she thinks that you were acting pricy and snooty because her boyfriend had asked you out before her. (It came down to boys every time.)
- Worst of all, those guys still tried to flirt with you; and you know you can't say anything to your friend because either she would believe you and end up being heartbroken for months or would not believe you and say that you were just jealous and wanted her to breakup with her bf. Ha! As if!

It was and is a no win situation.

'Let's go. What are we waiting for?' said Lilly.

Bella and Leila were digging into burgers. Celia, Lilly and Savera were eating some sort of beef pickle. Eww! Beef pickle! Tiana glared at them. They noticed the look on Tiana's face and burst out laughing. All of them were sitting on their beds in their new dormitory. This year, their dorms were much bigger. There was less privacy but more fun. Their beds were together. Leila's bed was on Tiana's right and Bella's was on her left. The rest were in front of their beds. They had reached their school in the afternoon and it was almost dinner time now. They had already changed from their skirts into their warm track suits because it was freezing cold in the hills. Despite the cold, Tiana loved her school. It had made her strong. It had taught her to survive when she was thrown into rough waters and to have fun at the same time. The only drawback was that they had to do all their work themselves. From making beds to polishing their shoes and waking up early, you were responsible for everything. Except for these reasons, Tiana loved Hill View. Sure she missed the luxuries of home, but she had made friends who she knew would be by her side for a lifetime; and she would always be thankful for that.

'Tiana, all of us will always eat non-veg. You have to accept it,' said Lilly.

'Can you at least avoid it in front of me?' asked Tiana.

'But you are always with us,' protested Savera.

'You are eating a dead cow,' grumbled Tiana, making a face which caused a barrel of laughter.

'Thank God it is dead otherwise I don't think I could have eaten it,' laughed Savera. This absurd retort made Tiana smile too.

She gave up. She had no choice but to accept the fact that she was stuck between people with terrible tastes in food. Besides, she had had this conversation with her friends a zillion times . . . of course . . . always in vain.

'I am not really looking forward to dinner,' said Tiana, almost to herself.

'Why? It will be so much fun seeing the rest of our classmates after holidays. I have so much to tell all of them,' said Bella excitedly.

Tiana still hadn't got a chance to tell Bella or Leila about what had happened with Veer. Even thinking about it made her feel so uncomfortable. What was she supposed to say to Bella? And most importantly, would Bella believe her? Veer was the last thing that she wanted between her friendship with Bella. And she didn't want to go for dinner because she didn't want to see that git again.

'You are right. Dinner will be fun,' said Tiana in a tired voice.

There was something else that was bothering her. She had found out that her friends already knew about what kind of food they liked. Bella, Leila and Aliya love Italian. Celia and Savera like Chinese. And Lilly was devoted to McDonald's . . . which brings us back to square one. Tiana did not know or was not sure about her choice in food. She was a vegetarian for sure, but that was all she knew. Generally, she just ate whatever her friends suggested. She never gave it a serious thought. Anyway, she would find that out soon. It couldn't be so difficult. They heard the distant sound of the school bell indicating the time for dinner. Holidays were definitely over. Here they were again, taking their orders from a bell!

Dinner meant meeting the rest of their batch mates after almost two months.

The way some of the girls hug and kiss each other was so funny and oh so fake. Most of them did not even like each other, and the moment they turned their backs, they began their uninterrupted bitching again. Gossip kicked off every new term. Everyone had something new to say after the holidays. This was just the beginning. It would continue for the rest of the term. And as Tiana's friends were considered 'cool' (even more so now), they were talked about the most. She had already heard a few girls tell each other that Bella had coloured her hair and it didn't suit her. Girls admired Bella but at the same time, they were green with envy. Another bunch of girls was pondering over what Leila would do, as her boyfriend has passed out from school.

Tiana could no longer control her smile. Gossip was the main fodder for these girls and even boys! They practically lived on spreading rumors. The fate of every boy or girl in school depended on whether they were on the 'right' or 'wrong' side. We all now know very well as to what 'right' and 'wrong' means. Tiana knew that more than anyone. Friends changed for boys. Okay, so they were an important part of growing up but the way the girls started revolving their lives around them was just so stupid. They were of course the hottest topic of discussion in the dormitories.

Tiana was grateful that all seven of them had managed to stay friends for so long. She had seen best friends break up for a guy. No chance of that happening with them, thought Tiana gladly, considering her best friend was going out with her brother. She had decided a long time back that she would never let a guy wreck her relation with any of her friends. It was true. She had already dodged a million embarrassing requests for dating a guy because she knew that one of her friends was interested in him. Not that it was a big sacrifice . . . she didn't really like them. She just followed her principle of staying out of situations that one would regret later.

In the dining hall, their table was right at the centre and was crowded. It was just in front of the main entrance, which meant that Tiana and her friends could catch most of the action during meal time. All kinds of things happened during the meals. Students being punished for various reasons, guests of the school or ex-students coming to visit, teachers fighting or gossiping (yes, even teachers did that; only differance was that they fought about boring things like substitutions). But their gossip was sometimes even more interesting than that of the students. Teachers made many important decisions during lunch and the students always managed to catch snippets of their conversations.

Apart from her own gang of eleven, a lot of guys sat at their table and that made it a very rowdy one.

Tonight, as usual, the maximum amount of noise was coming from her table. Everyone was seated, and only her place was vacant. Everybody was talking about something very excitedly when she reached the table and took her seat between Zain the brain (Aliya's boyfriend) and Leila. The moment they noticed that Tiana was amongst them, they stopped talking. There was something positively fishy about this sudden silence. What was going on, she thought, getting a little uncomfortable because everyone was avoiding looking in her direction. The creepy feeling of knowing that you are into some sort of a mess slowly started marching in her mind.

'What's wrong guys? Why are you acting so strange?' asked Tiana anxiously.

'Is it true Tiana?' demanded Bella, tearfully.

'Is what true Bella?' asked Tiana, puzzled to see her cry. She felt like she had been magically transferred into one of the ridiculous soaps that have flooded the television channels nowadays.

'I don't believe it! How could you do this to me?' cried Bella.

By now, the entire table was looking at both of them with a lot of interest. Nothing could beat the fun of witnessing an argument of such nature . . . it was the perfect ingredient to spice up life in a boarding school. Tiana looked helplessly at Leila. She tried to give her a comforting look. Only Leila's and Aliya's expressions looked empathetic. Out of the corner of her eye, Tiana noticed that Veer was smirking at her.

'Will somebody please tell me what is going on?' asked Tiana, becoming more and more confused.

'Don't try to act innocent Tiana. Veer told us what happened between the two of you,' cried out Bella.

'Oh! He did. Did he?' said Tiana, looking foxed. 'Then why are you getting angry with me?'

'I don't believe it! You came on to my boyfriend. Asked him to dump me and go out with you. Did you honestly think that Veer won't tell me! And now, you have the cheek to ask me why I'm getting angry with you!' said Bella through gritted teeth.

'What?' Tiana couldn't believe that she just heard those ridiculous words.

So this was what it was all about. A lie that Veer has come up with to save his ass and pricked ego. Worse, Bella actually believed him! Veer the sneak was actually out on a mission to spoil her friendship with Bella! Everyone except Leila and Aliya believed him. That is what they had been gossiping about. By the next morning, the entire school will be feeding on this piece of gossip which would have donned an added layer of garnishing by then! Why couldn't she have a normal beginning to the term? If people were going to talk about her, could not the topic be her hair or weight? Why a lie that that pest Veer had made up? Taina could see the greedy glint in the eyes of all the students sitting around them . . . the glint that was asking for a catfight . . . Veer's were the hungriest! No! She was not going to let them have what they wanted and therefore, very wisely, chose not to give any justification.

'If you all really think that I could stoop so low,' said Tiana, looking at all her friends with contempt and then resting her eyes on Bella before continuing, 'and that too for a guy I HATE, then I feel embarrassed to call you my friends. You have insulted me and friends don't do things like this to each other,' finished Tiana, in a calm and dignified tone. With that, she got up and left the table. Getting to see the stunned look on Veer's face gave her immense satisfaction. Not like he had imagined, she thought wryly. He must have expected her to go ballistic like she had the other night. He must have thought that she'll get upset and angry. Tough luck dim-wit! On the contrary, she was not upset at all. Now that she no longer cared about what others thought and about being with the 'cool people', she felt a burden rising from her shoulders.

She no longer felt the need to please others in order to fit in. To hell with such friends if they were ready to believe atrocious stuff about her. And all this after so many years of supposed friendship. They were so touchy about everything and wanted reassurances through false opinions. She could make new friends, but she would not explain or justify herself to anyone. On her way out, she ran into Karam.

'How come you're leaving so soon? Finished with your dinner?' asked Karam.

Apparently, the rumour hadn't reached his ears yet. Would he believe her or would he act like the rest? That shall be found out soon. It was testing time for all those who she thought were her friends.

'Ask the people on my table why I left. Good night!' said Tiana and walked back to the dorms.

Back in the dorms, she had just finished unpacking and setting up her cupboard when Leila came and sat on her bed.

'I need you to know that I believe you. I know you would never do this to a friend and that too for a slob like Veer. Bella must be crazy. Yuck!' said Leila and made a face.

'I know that Leila. Thanks for believing me,' replied Tiana gratefully.

Just then, Aliya and Savera popped in and vouched for the same opinion. It felt so good to know that the people who mattered believed her even without her giving an explanation.

'Thank you so much guys! It means the world to me that you feel this way about me,' said Tiana. 'Do you want to know what happened exactly?'

'Something happened?' asked Savera, her eyes becoming rounder with curiosity.

'Yes.'

Then she related the entire episode to them.

'What an asshole! He is so cheap, T,' said Leila in disbelief.

'And he put the entire blame on you!' exclaimed Aliya angrily.

'The way you handled the situation in the dining hall was great Tia. I can understand now how angry you must have been but you spoke so coolly and calmly. We are so proud of you,' beamed Savera, sounding very impressed.

In a little while, the rest of the girls filled up the dorms. Bella came in just as the dorms were about to get locked. Bella's bed was next to Tiana's and Bella did everything she could to avoid looking at her. That suited Tiana just fine. She changed into her nightdress and walked across the dorms to go to the bathroom. She could not help but notice that there were whispers following her. Gossip, rumours . . . she had forgotten about what it felt like to be talked about behind your back. Even if all the troubled waters that were raging between her and Bella ever calmed down, things won't be the same ever again. Tiana could and would not trust her the way she used to. The nagging sound of stalking whispers was irritating Tiana. Tiana turned around to glare and caught a bunch of junior girls red-handed . . . they were pointing at her! They got embarrassed at being caught and scurried away in different directions.

She returned to her bed and found Leila sitting on it.

'First night of the new term and two of you are not even looking at each other, what fun!' said Leila, sounding disheartened.

'I am sorry I have spoiled the fun,' said Tiana.

'It is not your fault. It is the fault of your good looks,' smiled Leila.

'What are you talking about?' asked Tiana warily.

'If you hadn't been so good looking, Veer wouldn't have liked you. You wouldn't have refused him and he wouldn't have become jealous,' said Leila, lazily yawning by the end of her sentence.

'And you wouldn't have lost your mind!' smiled Tiana.

'It is true,' said Leila.

'Yes, in a very bizarre way, you do make sense Leila,' reflected Tiana.

'Bella is not talking to Aliya, Savera and me either,' complained Leila.

'What? Why? Because you guys believe me? I am so sorry for that Leila.' Tiana felt and looked startled at the fact that Bella was behaving in such an immature way.

'Don't be sorry. She'll start feeling sorry super soon . . . i.e. when she gets to find out the truth. Lilly and Celia are taking Bella's side. They'll be sorry too,' said Leila.

Tiana felt terrible. This was the last thing she had ever wanted—to divide her friends into gangs of supporters and opposers. But what could she do now? It was not entirely her fault.

'I think we should go to sleep. We have to get up early tomorrow, and Karam has already warned me about the long lectures waiting for us,' smiled Leila.

'Yes, he warned me too. I hope they are not as bad as he makes them seem. Anyway, good night girls!'

On the first day of the classes, the students were divided into new sections and got their new books. Leila, Aliya and Bella were with Tiana for all the subjects. The entire gang (if you can call them that) was together for the English classes. This year (as Karam had already warned them), the teachers gave them long lectures about the importance of the Boards. They got an earful about the life-defining and life-changing exams. Your future depended upon it. Be serious, blah! blah! Seven classes. Seven different teachers and all of them repeating the same stuff in their own ways. Didn't the teachers ever get bored of the continuous, predictable repetition of the same old stuff in each and every class, every year?

Till last year, it was the dress rehearsal—they said that you were in a pre-board class and next year you would be in the Board class and you would need to become more serious.

This year, they say that you are in the Board class. Next year, we would again be in a pre-board class, and so on and so forth. It was just unwanted over-hyped drama. Tiana and Leila were so sick of this hullabaloo that they could kill the next person who discussed Boards. It was just the first day of classes and people were already getting panicky and nervous. Some had already started reading from extra guides and were discussing tuition notes. At times, all this made Tiana feel very insecure. She hadn't thought that her classmates would behave like lunatics on the very first day of the term. This was madness. Soon, either she would start behaving like them or would not allow all this to bother her mental peace and balance.

Things with Bella were not improving either. Both of them were ignoring each other completely in the dorms, in class and even at the dining table. Didn't Veer feel guilty? Didn't he have a conscience? Probably not. Even at this moment, he must be acting like the town crier and boasting in front of someone about how Tiana begged him to go out with her. Some day he will pay for his wicked ways, thought Tiana, bitterly hoping that that day would come soon.

Surprisingly, that day came at super-sonic speed. During lunch, astonishingly, Bella apologised.

'What did you just say?' asked Tiana, not able to believe her ears.

'I am sorry Tiana. I should have asked you what had actually happened before blaming you on the house. I am sorry,' said the guilty looking Bella.

'What changed your mind so suddenly?' asked Tiana, miffed by the sudden change in behaviour.

'Karam of course,' said Bella, 'didn't he tell you?'

'Tell me what?' asked Tiana. What did Karam know that she didn't?

'He was there when Veer came on to you. You didn't see him because he was in the kitchen, but he saw and heard everything. He came and told me all this before lunch,' explained Bella.

Wow! For the first time, she stood up for herself and everything fell into place automatically! It felt so good. If only she had started this 'finding it' a little earlier. Her next thoughts were on Veer. A bitter-sweet smile lit up her face. She had been proved right. How she wished to see his face now! Very appropriately, he was missing from the table. On the other hand, Bella had needed reassurance from somebody else—a guy—before she could believe the truth about Tiana. Couldn't she have gone by her instincts and trusted her friend? That was what had hurt Tiana the most.

'It is okay Bella. I really don't care,' shrugged Tiana.

'I really am sorry,' insisted Bella. Then she looked at Leila, Aliya and Savera and apologised to them too.

Tiana had expected this episode to go on forever. But thanks to Karam, things were normal again. She spotted Karam leaving the dining hall and excused herself from the table.

'Hey, thanks for sorting my problem,' said Tiana gratefully.

He turned to look at her and smiled.

'No problem. I was there when Veer was talking about all that crazy stuff. I was going to come out and help you but you did a good job.'

'Thank you so much!' replied Tiana.

'I would have revealed the truth last night but I just found out about it before lunch, when I heard Veer discuss it with some guys. You must have noticed that he was not present for lunch,' said Karam.

'Yes I did. Where is he?' questioned Tiana.

'In the hospital,' came the quick reply.

She felt so glad at this news. Let Veer come out of hiding. Then she would tackle him.

'Are things fine with Bella?' asked Karam.

'They will be. But I am not sure if I can forget this entire thing so easily,' replied Tiana honestly.

'I understand. But just a piece of advice. Don't hold any grudges. Everyone makes a mistake,' said Karam, with seriousness in his tone.

'I'll try,' laughed Tiana. She was just too happy and satisfied to be serious.

Karam just arched his eyebrows and left.

While walking back to the dorms, Leila caught up with her.

'My brother was useful for once at least. I wonder where Mr Veer is?' laughed Leila.

'In the hospital,' smirked Tiana.

'Oh! T, you scared him so much that he is hiding in the hospital!' said Leila, in mocking concern.

'What can I say? He asked for it,' replied Tiana in the same tone.

They were walking or rather crawling with their very heavy bags on their backs.

'It's the first day of the term and we already have so much prep to do. This year will suck,' moaned Leila.

'Yes, it will. Teachers have not even finished the first chapter of the course and half the people have already started solving sample papers,' added Tiana.

'I just hope we can cope up with all this,' sighed Leila.

✧

Now that Tiana and Bella were on talking terms again, the atmosphere in the dorms was much better. All of them were sitting together and talking about the first day of classes when all of a sudden, Leila started to cry. Now what was this all about? Leila was supposed to be the mature and mentally strong one amongst them. She rarely cried. This meant that something was really bothering her.

'Leila, what's wrong? Why are you crying?' asked Bella.

'Nothing [sniff], I am sorry to bother you like this. I am fine [sniff],' sobbed Leila.

'Hey, something is definitely wrong Leila. Come on . . . tell us,' said Tiana, concerned about her friend.

The past two days had been a roller-coaster ride for her. First, Veer coming on to her, Bella blaming her for what was not her fault, all the false rumours, and then, all this drama about the Boards . . . one horrible incident after another. Now Leila, of all people, crying! This was becoming too much to handle.

'I don't think I should tell you. You guys will just laugh,' sniffed Leila.

'Don't be ridiculous Leila. We won't laugh, we promise,' said Tiana.

'Promise.'

'Promise.'

Leila took a deep breath and said, 'I am missing Sid.'

Oh no! Tiana had absolutely forgotten about how Leila would be feeling now that Sid was no longer in school. How could she be so insensitive to Leila's feelings? Sid must be missing her too. They had been inseparable (much to Tiana's disgust). Now they were so far away from each other. But there was nothing that Tiana could do to help Leila. She hadn't seen this coming.

'I know I am sounding all whiny and irritating but I just miss him so much!' sobbed Leila.

'You don't sound whiny, understand? I am sorry I didn't realise that you would miss him so much Leila. Is there anything we can do to cheer you up?' asked Tiana. Deserting sources of ideas during crises . . . that's Tiana . . . couldn't think of a way herself, so asked Leila instead!

'Can we get out of this dorm? I am really getting irritated seeing those two girls studying,' replied Leila, smiling between tears.

'Of course we can get out of here. Even I feel like murdering those two girls,' replied Savera, which was funny because Savera loved to study.

All of them left the dormitory and headed for the school cafeteria—a place where they spent most of their free time and sometimes even sneaked into when they were not supposed to be there. Today was one of those days. The temptation to sneak into the cafeteria at that thrilling hour persuaded them to risk it. But if they got caught, that too on the first day of the term, the outcome wouldn't be very cheerful. As it is, Tiana and her friends kept getting into trouble every other day. Reasons varied from being rude to teachers, missing classes, forgetting to bring text books to class, incomplete prep (the most regular one), fighting with boys, to lights being on after lights out, unpolished shoes, long nails, etc. etc. It seemed as if whatever they did, even by mistake, got them into trouble with the teachers. So now, their new course of action was – if you are destined to get in trouble, might as well get in trouble for really worthwhile things . . . like sneaking into the café.

All of them took their favourite table. The wafting aroma of brownies and muffins automatically made them realise that they were very hungry. Tiana was happy to notice that Leila was back to being her bright and chirpy self again. Confiding in them had surely helped her feel better. At least she wasn't crying and soon, both Sid and Leila would get used to staying apart. They didn't have any choice.

'I know what kind of food I like,' said Tiana, surprising everyone with this odd statement. At first, they looked confused but then they realised that this was her 'finding it' quest.

'So what are you waiting for? Tell us,' said Savera.

'Let me guess. It's Italian right?' asked Bella, hopefully.

'It is Indian,' said Tiana simply.

'What? You like Indian more than any other cuisine?' asked Bella and Savera, unable to believe what they just heard.

Her friends thought that having a 'taste' for exotic foreign cuisines was what made them cool. Liking Indian food was like sacrilege . . . no way . . . not acceptable! They looked at her as if she was the mad March hare from *Alice in Wonderland*! Though they were shocked into silence, their dumb-founded expressions said it all!

In normal circumstances, she would have lied and said that she liked Italian. It was cool to like cosmopolitan cuisines. But now, things were different. Tiana was done with lying. As she got out of her bed this morning, she realised that she actually loved Indian food. Not just because of its taste but because of the memories connected with it. Its aroma reminded Tiana of her childhood . . . the family holidays. Her mom was an amazing cook (that is, when she cooked). They were very heartwarming memories and all she had to do was to smell the delicious rajma chawal to get all nostalgic and transported into childhood. No doubt, the Indian cuisine was her favourite. She was surprised that she hadn't even considered Indian food as a possibility. All these false tastes were only due to the influence of her friends who were busy chasing other cultures. They probably felt that what they already were and had was not good enough, thought Tiana. How could she explain this to them?

'I don't see why it should be shocking if an Indian likes Indian food Bella? I'm done with lying and this is the first time in ages that I am speaking truthfully,' said Tiana, glaring at Bella as if daring Bella to come up with an argument against her.

Bella was smart enough to keep quiet. Just then, Celia and Lilly came bursting through the café door.

'We thought we would find you here,' said Lilly excitedly.

Glad because of the diversion from the dangerously nearing argument, Bella quickly asked Lilly about what was happening.

'Guess what is happening this Saturday?' asked Lilly.

'The Kick Off Social,' replied Tiana, boredom written all over her face.

'How did you find out? It was just announced,' said Lilly, disappointed that Tiana already knew and spoiled her 'breaking-news' broadcast.

'Because it happens every year silly! You don't have to be a genius to figure that out,' replied Tiana.

But before Lilly could answer that, a couple of junior girls sitting by the door squeaked and scampered to the back door.

'What's wrong?' asked Leila.

'Senior mistress coming down the slope,' came the whispered scream.

For a second, they observed shocked silence while they stared at each other with question marks and exclamation marks written all over their faces. And then . . . 'Heck! RUN!' yelled Leila.

They ran through the back door in panic. Who wanted to get in trouble on the very first day? Once outside, they had only two routes to follow – one was to go to the front and face their senior mistress, who completely hated all of them and would be delighted to punish them; and the second one was to climb down a khud (slope). They chose the khud.

What followed could surely give our Bollywood action-comic scenes a run for their money!

First, Bella crossed over the railing and tried to climb down. The rest of them followed. It was a tough job. Tiana nearly slipped but she caught hold of a bush and balanced herself again. But by doing this, a lot of pebbles skittered downhill and hit Savera on her head. Bella slipped twice and landed on the road with a twisted ankle; Leila had hurt her knee; and Tiana had a scratched elbow by the time they reached the road below. Just then, they heard their senior mistress's voice. She was standing by the railing where all of them had been a few moments ago! It was as if she knew that they had been climbing down the slope. But she couldn't see them because they were well hidden underneath a large bush. The girls below held on to all their powers of tolerance to keep themselves from uttering a single scream of pain or even catching their breath. Savera could actually imagine little Tweeties hovering over her head! Once they heard the senior mistress' voice fade away, they ran from their hiding zone . . . except for Bella, who was limping.

'My God! That was the craziest thing I have ever done,' panted Leila.

'Desperate times call for desperate measures,' replied Aliya.

'I think she knew that we were sneaking away,' joined in Savera.

'Of course she knew! Or else she wouldn't have come to look down the khud,' said Tiana thoughtfully.

'And if by any stroke of luck, she doesn't come to know of our escapade of her own accord, she can surely put two and two together when she sees your wounds,' said Celia.

'Yeah, like it was my dream to sprain my ankle,' said Bella sarcastically.

'But Celia has got a point Bella. Leila and Tiana can hide their cuts but we will have to cook up a story for you in case any teacher asks us what happened,' said Savera. 'Now we need to take all three of you to the hospital.'

'No,' snapped Bella.

'Why, your sprain will become worse if you don't,' said Savera with the I-know-what-is-right look.

'I don't want to go to the hospital,' insisted Bella.

Tiana understood what was bothering Bella. Veer had been admitted (or rather acted his creepy way into getting admitted) to the hospital and Bella had just broken up with him. It would be painful for her to see him. Especially because now Bella knew what a rat he really was.

'Bella, you need to show your ankle to the doctor,' whispered Tiana into her ear, 'I will make sure that Veer stays out of your way.'

'Thanks!' she whispered, gratefully.

Thanks to the limping Bella and Leila, they reached the hospital at turtle speed.

'I will go check where Veer is. Then you all can come inside,' offered Tiana.

'No wait, let me go. You might just start fighting with him again and the hospital is not the place for another confrontation,' smiled Savera.

She left them outside and after five minutes, signaled them to come in.

'Where is he?' asked Bella nervously, while the nurse cleaned up Leila's and Tiana's cuts.

'Boy's ward. He wants to talk to you but I told him to stick to his bed or else he would have to face Tiana again. He decided to stay in,' replied Savera, grinning from ear to ear at Tiana.

'Seems like I have been successful in shaking your ex-boyfriend out of his over-sized ego and MCP-ism,' said Tiana in a pained voice, as the nurse was dabbing cotton dipped in anti-septic on her cuts.

'These days you seem to be leaving a great impact on everyone, T,' said Leila.

That meant that the change in her was noticeable, thought Tiana happily.

'That's me!' sang Tiana. She was feeling unusually happy. For some reason, she felt that this term would turn out to be great for her.

༄

Tiana could hear a faint thud. Slowly, the banging grew louder and woke her up from her deep slumber. Someone was knocking at her bedroom door yet again. Why could they not leave her alone? She forced herself out of the bed while the previous nights' events came rushing back to her. She checked the time. 5 pm. She had been sleeping for over eleven hours. She got up to unlock the door. Her mother and Sid had been waiting patiently outside her door.

'Tia, thank God you finally opened the door! Are you alright honey?' asked her mother anxiously.

'Tiana, you have been in that room for so long. Come downstairs and eat something,' said Sid, equally anxious.

Eat. How could she eat? She was reminded of all the blood she had seen last night and felt dizzy. And so, for the first time in her life, Tiana blacked out . . .

FOUR

For the past two days, every girl in the dormitory had developed a freak obsession with clothes and make up. They had been trying out every imaginable kind of outfit in their spare time. Some had even started designing stuff with things that looked like rags to Tiana. They whispered about it during classes, during meals and even before sleeping. Tiana observed them, amused. You would think that they have been invited to the Queen's ball! From shoes to eye shadow . . . everything was just fussed over by the girls. It was just the start of term social, for God's sake! It's not like Tiana didn't believe in looking good. After all, she wanted to work in a fashion magazine. Looking good was important but the way some of these girls were behaving was just freaking unbearable. They tried on clothes every night after lights out and asked the same questions over and over again. 'How do I look? Do I look too fat? Does this fit? Don't you think it is tight around the waist?' Tiana had to put her pillow over her head to get some peace and quiet.

But there was something else that was creating a mild havoc in Tiana's mind at that moment. Something unexpected had happened the day before. While walking out of the dining hall after lunch, Karam caught up with her and asked her something which took her by surprise.

'Hi Tiana!'
'Oh! Hi Karam!'
'How is everything going on?'

'Great.'

Karam was fidgeting with his sweater sleeves. He had seemed a tad bit uncomfortable about something.

'Are you alright Karam?' Tiana asked, sensing that something was wrong.

'I was just wondering if you would . . . ,' hesitated Karam.

'If I would what?' asked Tiana curiously.

'No, forget it . . . Umm . . . actually I was just thinking . . . Would you like to go out with me and come with me to the Kick Off?' finished Karam, looking relieved and turning boiled beetroot red at the same time.

Oh no! Tiana freaked out mentally. Did Karam just ask her out?

'What? But I thought you were dating Jasmine?' replied the visibly stunned Tiana.

'Oh! I WAS. I broke up with her some time back,' he said, turning a shade darker. For a moment, Tiana felt that she even saw a shade of blue on his face! Before Tiana could say anything, Karam took the easy way out and said, 'You know what? Just forget what I asked you, okay? Please? Bye!' With that, he had walked away briskly.

Tiana was left dumbstruck. She had always thought of Karam as a good friend. Apparently, he liked her more than that. She didn't even know if she had handled this situation well enough. She didn't want to lose a friend because of what had just happened, but she had no clue how to sort out this mess either.

Tonight was the night, and the girls were extremely excited. Tiana was sitting on her bed but she could hear a couple of senior girls talking from a cubicle close to her bed.

'I think I should wear the pink top. Green makes me look fat,' whined one of them.

'Are you mad? Green looks much better on you. Besides, it is the IN colur at the moment,' said the other self-proclaimed fashion guru.

Tiana tuned out of their silly conversation as more fussing ensued. She had heard this kind of argument way too many times during the last few days and found it mind-numbingly boring.

Skirt or jeans?

Red or purple?

Heels or flats? Blah! Blah! Blah!

The worst part of all this was that the girls who were asking for advice had already made up their minds about what they were going to wear. Yet, they persisted or probably enjoyed going on and on about it. To ask for reassurance is one thing but this was just annoying. 'Do I look fat?' (nine out of ten times, this question is asked by the most slim girls), 'Am I looking too fat?' (mostly asked by the fattest girls), 'is it too vulgar', 'how is this color' and a million other worthless and useless questions were on the tip of every girl's tongue during the few days before the Kick Off.

Till last year, she would have lied to reassure them, but now that she had decided to be truthful to herself, why not be truthful to others. If they wanted to hear her opinion, then they would hear it. So if anyone asked Tiana for her advice, she replied truthfully. To the extra thin ones—'No, you are not looking fat but you look like a twig'. To the fat ones—'I am sorry but you look fat'. 'No, it does not look vulgar.' 'I don't like that colour. It does not suit you at all.'

Naturally, tasting bitter truth was not exactly the cuisine that the girls preferred. Now, no one dared to ask Tiana for her opinions.

'T, what have you been telling the girls? They are horrified by some of the things you said,' said Leila, coming up to her bed.

'They asked me what I thought and I told them,' came Tiana's innocent reply.

'So you told them what you really thought?' questioned Leila, narrowing her eyes on Tia.

'Yes, exactly what I thought,' replied Tiana, smiling at her friend.

'You can't do that!' exclaimed Leila, 'I mean, your "finding it" is for you, not those poor girls. They don't want to hear the truth.'

'They were asking for it, Leila. I was sick of their questions. And I personally think that they should get used to listening to the truth. You can't live in a bubble all your life,' said Tiana, trying to defend herself.

'Okay but I don't want everyone to hate my best friend either,' said Leila.

'That's the last thing on my mind,' replied Tiana.

'And the first on mine. Please, no more honesty is the best policy, okay?'

'Okay.' She gave in and got up to go and sit on Aliya's bed. Aliya was getting dressed.

'Hi Ali!' said Tiana, slumping onto Aliya's bed.

'Why aren't you getting dressed up?' asked Aliya.

'I am not even sure if I want to go,' said Tiana honestly. She didn't know how to face Karam after what had happened yesterday.

'Why? What's wrong with you? Just go and get dressed T,' said Aliya, pushing Tiana towards her bed where her clothes were lying.

'Fine, I will change,' said Tiana, as if resigning to unalterable fate.

The truth was that whatever had happened between Karam and her kept bugging her. She knew she could have handled it better than she had. But what had she done? She had made the situation more awkward for both of them. Till now, whenever anyone had asked her out, she had refused without thinking twice . . . and most of all, without getting upset about it. But it was different with Karam because he was already a good friend and Leila's brother. She still hadn't confided in Leila about what had happened.

She slipped into her black skirt and top and went into the room at the rear end of the dorms, where the rest of her friends were getting ready.

'Guys, are you ready?' asked Tiana.

'Yeah, we are done,' replied Bella slipping her feet into bright red shoes which matched her top. Her ankle had healed. It had turned out to be a mild sprain. One by one, they left the room and only Leila and Tiana were left.

'I am stuck with two people who refuse to go with anyone,' said Leila.

'Who is the second one?' asked Tiana.

'Karam, who else,' replied Leila, as if it was the most obvious thing.

Tiana's stomach lurched at Karam's name. Should she tell Leila about what had happened?

'I thought Karam was going out with Jasmine,' said Tiana, because she was sure that he was. If she had known that he had broken up with Jasmine then she would have behaved in a different way when Karam had asked her out.

'Which ancient century are you living in? Karam broke up with her at the end of last term,' replied Leila.

'Oh! I didn't know that. I mean, you didn't tell me either,' said Tiana, wishing that Leila had told her.

'As if you care about Karam's love life!'

Leila was right. Tiana didn't care about Karam's love life. After all, she was not interested in him at all and just liked him as a decent buddy, and her best friend's brother. At least she didn't till yesterday, when he asked her out and included her in his love life. She was still a little stunned because she had never seen this coming.

Why couldn't everything remain the same? She was convinced that she had hurt Karam's feelings. He had practically fled from her side yesterday. And today, he had not even said a friendly 'hi' to her in the dining hall . . . something he always did. She was just thankful that he was her senior, which meant that they would not be together in any of the classes.

Tiana was still confused by it though. Usually if any guy liked her, she used to find out either by the way he started behaving around her (extremely quiet or showing off excessively) or someone else always told her. This enabled her to handle the situation in a proper manner. Tiana knew that you needed to be polite to the guys when you were turning them down because they have massive egos and no good would come out by hurting them. But then, there were some guys who just didn't give up and pissed you off. This demanded a different kind of treatment which she knew only too well!

But she had not seen it coming from Karam. She was pretty sure that Karam had not told anyone about it either. No surprise that she had been caught off-guard. And now, the Kick Off was looming in front of her.

'Let's go,' urged Leila, looking into the mirror one last time and forcing Tia to come out of her train of thoughts.

'Ya, let's go.'

∽

The Kick Off was a school ritual that marked the start of the new term. It was held in the school gymnasium which was stuffy and stinky. Even though it was freezing cold outside, the moment Tiana entered the hall, she started feeling sticky and hot. She really was not in a party mood, unlike her friends who had already started dancing. Bella was cheerful again. The news of her break-up with Veer had reached the eager ears of all the boys. They were all very excited and at least five had already asked her out in the last two days. Well, you know girls love it when something like this happens. It makes them feel like the princesses they always wanted to be. She was pretty much over Veer.

Tiana stayed with all of them for half-an-hour but after that, she went to the corner benches and sat down. Even though she had hardly danced, she was feeling very tired. She was massaging her feet when she heard Karam's voice. She looked up and saw him. He was standing right in front of her. She could feel her tongue forming a knot! She didn't know what to say so she just said hi.

'Hi!' replied Karam, 'Tiana, about what I asked you yesterday . . . '

Before he could finish his attempt at a sentence, Tiana spoke. 'It's okay Karam. I will forget about it.' Tiana had just started to feel victorious for her ability to make things easier for both of them and that this would be the end of the matter, when Karam comes up with another one of his cause-to-make-mouth-drop-on-the-floor statements.

'No! Actually I wasn't going to say that,' said Karam, a little hesitantly.

'Oh! Sorry, please go on,' said Tiana, feeling a little somersault in her tummy.

She could feel it coming . . . the moment where you don't know what to do . . . what to say . . . where you're only speaking in your silly interior monologue! She was definitely not ready for this part right now. In fact, it was the last thing she wanted to do. But much to her disappointment, Karam did go on and what he said was the last thing she wanted to hear.

'Tiana, it is kind of weird saying this to you,' he went on, 'because you are a really good friend . . . but I like you a lot more than just a friend Tia.'

Oh no! The moment is here! What was she supposed to say to that? Tiana was pretty sure that she thought of Karam only as a friend and didn't want any sort of awkwardness creep in between them. Interior monologue: Why am I always destined to get stuck in such a wretched situation? Okay, will figure out destiny later . . . first find your tongue woman!

[gulp] 'Karam, all this is very sudden for me and I just . . . '

'Wait. I know it is sudden for you but I just had to tell you because I have hidden it for quite some time now. And if you don't feel the same way, it is alright. I hope we can still stay friends,' said Karam quickly.

'I hope so too,' replied Tiana, relieved that Karam himself had the brains to give her the option. Usually, this option never enters the empty recesses of the tiny brains of most boys. Karam was just about to say something when Bella came and sat on the chair beside her.

'It is so hot. There is no place to even stand, forget about dancing,' whined Bella.

'Come on Bella, you are enjoying yourself. What with all the attention you are getting from so many boys,' smiled Karam.

This cheered up Bella considerably. It was as if she had forgotten that she was getting so much attention and Karan just helped her recall the wonderful moments of exclusive attention.

'Excuse me gals, I have to go find my friends,' said Karam and without looking at Tiana, scurried off. Yeah! Sure they could stay friends. It was getting so awkward already. God! What was she going to do?

'Why aren't you dancing?' asked Bella.

'My feet are hurting and I am not in the mood to party.'

'Come on! You can't fool me,' said Bella, with a I-know-what-you're-hiding look.

Now what was Bella talking about?

'What? About why am I sitting here?' asked Tiana, looking confused.

'Because you wanted to sneak a few minutes alone with your loverboy!' said Bella.

Tiana was not sure if she had heard it right. What did Bella just say?

'WHAT?' The reaction time was a little late but Tiana was shocked nevertheless.

'You know,' said Bella knowingly.

'Know what?' asked Tiana, in the snappiest of voices.

'What I know,' said Bella, bringing in mystery into her voice. she knew it and she was enjoying and taking advantage of every moment of her knowing it! Sometimes she could be a real pain, thought Tiana.

'What do you know?' Tiana was getting impatient now.

'Okay chill! I know that you like Karam. I mean, whenever I turn to look for you in between classes or during meals in the dining hall, and even tonight, I have always found you talking to him. I just thought something might be going on.'

Great! Now Bella thinks that she likes Karam. Could this night become worse than worst?

'Bella, it is not what you think,' sighed Tiana.

'It is okay. I won't tell anyone. Especially not Leila because if Leila finds out, it might be a tad bit difficult for you,' said Bella matter-of-factly.

'Why is that?'

'Because Karam is her brother. And you weren't very supportive about her liking Sid. So why will she be supportive about you liking Karam?' said Bella.

Yes, this night was on its way to become a live nightmare. Obviously, Bella had given this entire situation a lot of thought and she was right. Maybe even Leila will freak out the way she had freaked. The only difference in this situation was that Tiana didn't like Karam. He liked her. And she was not going to go out with him. So maybe, Leila won't freak. But Tiana had made up her mind. She was going to tell Leila about everything. She didn't want things to become weird and uncomfortable between her and Leila.

'Bella, there is nothing to hide. I don't like Karam,' said Tiana, trying one last time to make Bella understand the truth. But Bella had made up her mind to believe what she wanted to believe in. And after five minutes of idle chat, some senior guy came and took Bella along with him. Tiana was left alone again.

She was really feeling tired now. The first week of the new term had really been hectic. After two months of lazy holidaying, moulding yourself into the disciplined school mode was very tiring. The very first day had been impossible to cope up with. Their senior mistress had finally figured out that they had sneaked into the cafeteria. What followed was detention for three days after their classes. What's more . . . the prep kept piling up into Himalayan heaps. Every teacher had given them a lot of work. All their pleas to reduce the overloading prep fell upon deaf ears. Class ten was turning out to be a real drag.

Tiana decided to leave the party. It was finally the weekend and she wanted to catch up on sleep. For the past one week, they had been staying up late at night, finishing their prep or just sitting and talking. But to get up early the next morning was a struggle . . . especially when their matron started screaming and tugging at their quilts. Who wants to wake up to the shrill ear-piercing sounds of 'get up girls!'? Yup . . . they had to . . . and this was just the tip of the iceberg. Now that the weekend had finally arrived . . . after what seemed like centuries . . . they could sleep as much as they wanted to.

Without telling her friends, Tiana made a quick exit from the gym. The moment she stepped out, a blast of the freezing cold wind took her breath away for a moment. She wrapped her shrug tightly around her and slowly started walking towards the dorms.

∽

Tiana got up on Sunday morning feeling fresh and chirpy for the first time since coming to school. Her friends on the other side were not budging out of their beds. Obviously, they had slept late. Finally, she managed to drag them out just in time for breakfast.

'I really want to sleep some more,' groaned Lilly.

'Why did I stay up so late?' Leila was wondering aloud to herself.

They were sitting at the breakfast table and everyone except Tiana was feeling sleepy.

'Come on, you can catch up on your sleep later. Now let's go to the café,' urged Tiana.

She was getting bored sitting and listening to their whining. Finally, they had a day to themselves sans classes . . . and instead of soaking up the winter sun, they were sitting inside the dining hall.

'Please, let's go outside. It's deliciously sunny and anytime better than this cold hall,' said Tiana, getting up from her chair.

When she noticed that no one else was doing the same, she pulled Leila's chair. Leila, whose face was hidden in her hands, had not seen this coming and she got up with a start.

'What the hell!' yelled Leila, looking up and glaring at Tiana. Unfortunately for Leila, a teacher was standing close to their table.

'Leila, the dining hall is not the place for shrieking . . . and especially not for swearing. Behave like a lady!' commanded their math's teacher.

'Thanks a lot! My dream of starting my Sunday getting scolded by some irritating teacher has finally come true!' muttered Leila, sarcasm reeling through her voice.

'Oh God! I am sorry! Now let's go outside. Please!' begged Tiana.

'Yeah, let's. It is kind of cold in here,' agreed Aliya.

'Thank you!' said Tiana, looking gratefully at Aliya.

Slowly, everyone got up and left for the café. In all these years, this had been their Sunday ritual. In fact, it was so for everyone in the school. After Sunday breakfast (which they did not eat at all), they went to the school café and stayed there for as long as they could. Till class eight, Tiana and her friends used to spend a lot of time together on Sundays. But then, her friends started dating and Sunday mornings became a perfect time for them to date.

Believe it or not, dating was not allowed in their school – 'Strictly prohibited' as their senior mistress kept pointing out. But of course, this did not stop anyone from dating. Prohibited or not, Tiana had come to know that when her classmates wanted to do something, they would stop at nothing.

As far as Tiana's views were concerned, she thought that parents needed to understand that punishing, scolding or forcefully stopping their kids from doing something would not help. Parents and teachers keep getting pushy and the teenagers get even more defiant and rebellious. By the end of it, the teens just cut off their parents from their life and then, parents start thinking that their child had become prey to wrong habits and other imaginary possibilities. It kept getting messier. It's actually nobody's fault . . . yet, it's everybody's fault.

Anyway, everyone still dated, but they had to be very careful about it. Half the time, Tiana's friends kept getting into trouble because of their dating escapades. If any teacher even saw a girl talking to a boy, she would make a huge fuss about it. The girl then was unfortunately destined to a boring moral lecture session and the famous and highly intrusive five W's questionnaire—why, when, what, where and who!

The teachers in charge of the girls wanted a count of every minute, of every hour, and of every day. It could be so infuriating. It was already so difficult being a girl in this world . . . and to add to the misery, this difference in treatment and double standards had creeped into the supposedly unbiased walls of the school. If anything angered Tiana and her friends, it was that when a girl was caught dating, she was chewed up and sent off. But when it came to a guy, he was literately encouraged! It has happened in front of Tiana's very own eyes. Countless number of times!

Okay, Tiana understood the fact that girls needed to be more careful because they are . . . well . . . girls. But at least the guys shouldn't be encouraged. It's just not fair! The nerve of those teachers to do so, that too openly . . . in front of the girls! Male teachers obviously encouraged the boys by joking and saying stuff like 'good choice'. And the female teachers? They too joked about it in a 'boys will be boys' tone. Why this bias? Why do these dodgy blokes always get it easy? Did it ever occur to the teachers that a girl is required in order to date? If it is okay for a guy to date, then how can it not be okay for a girl You can't clap with one hand! And then they expect all that rubbish about 'respect your teachers' and blah blah! Why should respect be just from girls? Let those boys respect you as you clearly respect their feelings. Now to add on to the drudgery, the Boards were causing a dangerously increasing pile of prep work too. Tia's gang was certainly lagging behind. The rest of their classmates were way too ahead of them. Not only were they managing to finish their prep on time, they were also reading through the guides and extra reference material.

'I still haven't started those extra questions from the first chapter of English and Bio,' said Bella in a guilty tone.

Looks like prep is on everyone's mind, thought Tiana.

'It is okay, you can finish it today,' said Savera, trying to console the sincere Bella.

'But I wanted to sleep today,' complained Bella.

'You should have slept early Bella. Last night's Kick Off was very boring anyway,' said Tiana.

'Are you kidding me? It was not boring at all!' said Bella, suddenly forgetting that she was feeling sleepy at the mention of the Kick Off.

'Oh yeah! What's so great about a stinky gym?' asked Tiana.

'Tiana, you left early,' said Lilly.

'So?'

'So you missed all the action,' said Celia.

Apparently, Tiana had missed out on some things and she was pretty sure her friends were dying to tell her about whatever had happened.

'What action? What are you talking about?' asked Tiana, acting her part.

'You don't know any thing at all?' asked Bella.

'Out with it,' said Tiana. She was losing her patience now.

Bella and Celia looked very excited. Maybe because whatever had happened after Tiana left had been very amusing and they were going to relive it.

'So okay, here is what happened,' said Celia.

'It was so cool. I mean for me at least. I have never felt so important before,' joined in Bella, looking like she was on her way to cloud nine already.

'We were dancing right in the centre of the crowd,' said Lilly.

'And Bella was next to this senior guy. Suddenly, Veer came from nowhere!' said Celia excitedly.

'Yeah, I mean, I thought he was still in the hospital,' said Bella.

'But he came for the party,' said Lilly.

'Is this leading to something?' asked Tiana. She was put off by the fact that Veer will be coming to class on Monday as he had been discharged from the hospital.

'Yes it is. We are coming to the point,' said Lilly, a little annoyed that the story was not having the desired affect on Tiana.

'Well . . . Veer saw Bella talking to this other guy and he came up to Bella and asked if he could talk to her for a second. But Bella didn't want to talk to him,' said Leila.

'Yeah and this other guy pushed Veer. And Veer got very angry and punched him in the stomach. This happened right in the middle of the dance floor, in front of everyone,' added Lilly, speaking at super-sonic speed because of her excitement.

'What else can you expect out of a dud like Veer?' asked Tiana. She was not at all impressed. The 'action' she had missed was just Veer using a human punch bag.

'No Tiana, you still have not heard the best part,' squeaked Aliya.

'What's that?'

'After Veer punched that senior, that guy punched Veer back right on his nose. There was like a river of blood flowing out of his nose. There is a good chance that it is broken,' replied Aliya.

Now that was some good news! She should have been present when the 'river of blood' started to flow. This meant that Veer won't be in class on Monday either. Yes!

'That is really good news,' agreed Tiana.

'Even after that, they kept fighting. Finally Karam and Aryan had to stop them before any teacher could get a whiff of what was happening,' said Savera.

'Isn't it incredible? Two guys fought over me and are now admitted to the hospital. One for a broken nose and one for getting punched in the stomach!' Bella's drowsiness had gone for a toss!

'Yeah, great! Bella, now that you are completely awake, you won't have problems in finishing the prep,' said Tiana, taking advantage of the wide-awake look on Bella's face.

'What? Oh no! I will feel sleepy as soon as my excitement gets over,' replied Bella, matter-of-factly.

All the girls had a hearty laugh at her reply.

Even after this piece of literally breaking news, the gossip session refused to discontinue. It also brought out some other juicy snippets of information . . . something that Tiana had really missed out on.

'Tia, do you remember Karam's ex-girlfriend Jasmine?' asked Leila.

Why was Leila asking her about Karam's girlfriend? Does Leila know something? Tiana panicked as these questions zoomed in on her mind. For the past three days, even a mere mention of Karam's name made her feel uncomfortable.

'Yeah, of course I do. She is in our class,' said Tiana warily.

'She had the most embarrassing night ever,' stated Leila.

Relieved that Leila was not going to ask what Tiana had feared, she showed interest in this topic.

'Why what happened?' asked Tiana.

'She had borrowed my pink pumps for the party. And then she was showing them off in front of Jai, saying stuff like "I got them from Dubai during my holidays".' Jai was Leila's ex-boyfriend.

'So what's wrong with a little showing off?' asked Tiana.

'Tiana, Jai had given those shoes to me on our six month anniversary,' said Leila, as if it was a crime not to know such an 'important' piece of information.

'No kidding! Those shoes? Those cute pink ones? Oh no!' said Tiana.

'Yeah. And obviously Jai recognised them and since then, he's been acting like a jerk. He is telling everyone that Jasmine has been lying about going to Dubai during holidays and that she borrows shoes and clothes from other girls,' added Aliya.

'God! Poor girl! I mean, that must really suck,' said Tiana, feeling sorry for Jasmine.

'But who told her to go and show off?' said Bella coolly.

'Come on Bella. She is having a very tough time. I mean she has been crying since last night. And all these guys are joking about her very rudely, that too on her face,' said Savera. She was feeling sympathetic and hence was on the defensive side.

'Whatever!' muttered Bella, 'I think it was a very dumb thing to do. First borrow, then show off. That's so . . . so dumb,' finished Bella.

'Bella, just because you don't borrow clothes it does not mean that no one else feels the need to do so occasionally. Nobody is as rich as you,' replied Aliya.

Tiana could sense an argument on its way. Before Bella could get a chance to respond and make matters worse, Tiana stopped her.

'Okay, Jasmine is the one who should be getting defensive, not you, so please stop.' Tiana's firm voice worked . . . they stopped.

But Tiana was honestly feeling very bad for Jasmine. It must have been very embarrassing to be caught lying like this. Jasmine had already lost her boyfriend at the end of last term . . . and a break-up made a girl miserable. She had seen her friends after a break-up. It was definitely not a very nice sight. In fact, it was an ugly sight – puffy panda eyes, red noses, cranky mood swings, self-pity at its worst and a week, or perhaps a month in worse cases, of feeling utterly desolate and miserable. Jasmine had definitely become the joke of the week, maybe even the month.

Tiana spotted Jasmine sitting at a table near the main door. She went up to her to make her feel better. One thing that Tiana hated was seeing her friends miserable, especially when the cause of the misery was a boy.

'Hi Jasmine! I just want you to know that you can ask me to help you anytime if anyone tries to irritate you, okay?' said Tiana sympathetically.

Jasmine looked a little surprised by this offer but she seemed grateful for it too.

'Thanks Tia! It's just so embarrassing. Now everyone thinks that I don't own any clothes or shoes of my own. I have become the butt of ridicule,' cried Jasmine.

'Its okay. Public memory is short lived. Everyone will forget about it in a little while,' said Tiana.

'No, no one will forget it. I know,' wailed Jasmine.

Tiana tried to console her but it was no good. Jasmine kept on crying. So Tiana left her alone. Sometimes people just refuse to get out of the self-pity mode.

That was when Tiana realised another truth about herself. She hated self-pity. She believed in fighting back and not in sitting in a corner sobbing and despising oneself. Why should she deride herself? Everyone had bad days but we should never give up because of them. Sure, Tiana had had some embarrassing moments but till now she had never felt the need to hide away or die of embarrassment. That means that she really hadn't had too many embarrassing moments. Not that there weren't any but they weren't so bad either. She just wished that it would remain like that.

She went back to her friends' table.

'So how is she doing?' asked Aliya.

'I think she'll be fine,' replied Tiana.

'Exactly what did you tell her?' asked Savera.

'I told her that she can ask for my help if anyone pisses her off.'

'Why would you help her?' asked Bella, looking at Tiana as though she had gone bonkers.

'Because she is not in the state to fight back. And I think it will be very rude of us if we sit quietly and let the guys make fun of her.'

'Yeah, whatever!' It was quite evident that Bella cared two hoots about Jasmine's state.

It was almost noon, time for them to return to their dorms and start their prep. They got up and started to walk back. But once they reached their dorms, instead of doing their work they got into their cozy beds and dozed off. They were really tired. Even the usually restless and tireless Tiana was feeling the same. After sitting in the sun, she too had started feeling woozy. They decided that they would start their work after lunch. But after eating their lunch, they dropped off to sleep again. It was as if they had taken sleeping pills. So when Leila got up and checked the time, she freaked out because it was seven in the evening! She woke up the rest of them and showed them the time. One whole day wasted in sleeping! They could have easily finished their prep but now they would again have to stay up late to do it.

∽

'This just sucks,' said Tiana, 'I still have to finish my Math and Bio homework.'

'Same here,' said Bella.

It was Monday morning and they were walking from their dorms to their classes. Even though they had stayed up late the previous night, some work was still left. And now, they would have to take out time during classes to finish it. It had been like this for all the previous classes' prep too but they were supposed to be more serious in class ten, right? At least that's what the teachers had said on the first day. But old habits die hard. The moment they reached the classes' area, Tiana checked the time table and sighed in relief.

'Math and Bio are last and second last. Thank God! Bella, now we have enough time to finish it,' said Tiana, seeing a glimmer of hope.

'Thank God, really! I didn't want to be put in detention again,' replied Bella.

'Yeah, that would be the Monday morning blues limit,' said Tiana.

For now, they had a gloomy Monday of classes to look forward to. Class ten was turning out to be no easy ride.

Their first class was English. It had been a fun subject till last year but this year they had those lengthy poems in 'ye olde' English. Boring. Tiana and Leila sat together during classes on the last table of the last row. In front of them sat Bella and Aliya. It was their space. They had learnt that sitting in the back row had only pros, and no cons. They can easily understand everything that was being said, and yet were not under the painful scrutiny of the teachers' eagle-like eyes. It was a good place to sit and do whatever you want to do. Like finishing Bio prep. So while their English teacher was droning on about some nonsensical poem, they sneakily copied their prep from Savera's notebook. Yes, it was not a very honest thing to do. But who cares? Savera was a brain and it was very easy to read her handwriting. Anything that kept them out of detention would do. However, today, lady luck didn't seem to have them in her good books—the teacher caught them not paying attention. She came to their desks and noticed what was going on. She was so quick that they didn't even get time to hide their notebooks.

'Stand up all of you. Right now!' screamed their teacher.

They had no choice. They stood up reluctantly.

'Now get out!'

'Please ma'am,' requested Aliya.

'Go and stand next to the bell. Now!' snarled their teacher.

Oh no! Sending students to stand next to the bell was a very new trend which the teachers were following. If anyone did anything wrong, they were sent to the area near the bell. That area was crossed by all the senior teachers, visitors and even the headmaster as his office was just opposite the school bell. If you were made to stand there, everyone knew that you had done something wrong. Then, you got detention or any other imaginable punishment from the variety that all the teachers had up their sleeves. The bell was not a good place for students . . . except of course for the original notorious few who took pride in being recognised as official troublemakers.

'Ma'am please, we won't do this again,' pleaded Bella.

Standing by the bell, that too first thing on a Monday morning, was not exactly what the girls wanted for themselves. But Tiana knew that they had goofed up big time and there was no way of getting out of it now.

'Out! Right now!' repeated the teacher.

This time, the order was more of a scary scream! The girls grudgingly got up from their seats and went outside. It was chilly. They went and stood next to the bell. If any student crossed them, they would ask what had happened and would show their sympathy. Teachers asked too, but they weren't as kind. And to make things worse, their senior mistress showed up just when the class was about to get over.

'So Leila and company, back to your usual mischievous selves?' She looked at all of them for one grilling moment and then said, 'Detention on Sunday!' Happy with herself, she walked off. Her way of walking looked like a victory march!

'Great, now our Sunday is going to get spoilt,' cried Bella.

'Well, at least we will finish our work on time. Thanks to the detention,' said Tiana thoughtfully.

'Tiana, that is so not helping!' said Bella.

'Yeah, you are right. Next Sunday morning is wasted,' said Tiana.

By the time they reached the dining hall for breakfast, everyone knew that had landed themselves in detention.

'Laugh all you want, but it is just so irritating,' said Bella, feeling extremely frustrated.

'Why didn't you finish Bio yesterday?' asked Aryan.

'Because we went off to sleep,' replied Lilly.

'What? Then I think you deserve to be punished,' said Rehan, complacently.

'Are you out of your mind? How can you say such a rude thing? Who the hell do you think you are?' fired Tiana.

'Hey, relax Tiana. All I am saying is that we are in class ten after all. You all need to become serious,' replied Rehan.

'But we don't deserve to be punished,' said Leila, coolly.

'Oh, okay, okay! I am sorry. Relax Leila.'

Leila was saying something but Tiana was not paying any attention. She asked Leila to pass the water jug. Leila however, didn't respond.

'Leila, please pass me the water jug,' repeated Tiana.

But Leila was busy arguing with Rehan. So Tiana got up slightly from her chair and leaned to grab the jug. It was a little heavy because of which she flopped back on her chair with a lot of force. This however, turned out to be far too acrobatic a manoeuvre as her stupid chair lost its stupid balance and she FELL DOWN right in the middle of the dining hall! And to add the finishing touch, all the water from the jug that was in her hand spilt on her too.

Everyone was quiet for five seconds. The shock of the sudden fall made Tiana feel brain dead and bone deep miserable! All she could do was thank God for she was wearing pants and not a skirt! Oh thank God! The second probability was embarrassing to even imagine! After the customary observance of the five-second silence which usually comes after every shocking incident, the whole hall burst out into hysterical laughter. How rude! She looked like a cat which was just pulled out from a well! She could feel her face turning into a shade of burning red and her ears felt like they were the vents of a steam engine! All she could see was people rolling over with laughter. She was still on the wet floor when finally, Leila came to her aid.

'Tiana are you al . . . [stifled giggle] . . . right?' asked Leila, trying her level best to control the suppressed smile.

'Yes, I am grand. What do you think?' Tiana was getting highly irritated now. Even Leila was laughing . . . this was unbelievable!

'I am so sorry Tiana. But that was hilarious!' said Leila, bursting out into loud laughter now.

Tiana's head was hurting now. People were actually craning their necks to catch a glimpse of the source of entertainment. She ran her hand over the back of her head and felt a huge bump. That day has finally arrived. The day she wanted to die of embarrassment. In moments like these, Tiana wouldn't have minded if dinosaurs suddenly emerged and gobbled her up! At least she would have escaped this embarrassment! It was so humiliating. She picked up her chair and sat down.

'T, are you hurt?' asked Savera.

'I think you should go and change,' said Celia.

'Do you want me to come with you?' asked Bella.

'I think you should go to the hospital first,' added Leila.

'Guys let her breathe,' said Aliya.

Tiana was very still and quiet while her friends hovered around asking her all these questions. Maybe she was still in a state of shock. She just could not believe what had happened with her.

'Tiana . . . Tiana!' Leila was snapping her fingers too. Tiana didn't seem to notice.

'Are you listening to us, T?' asked Bella.

'Yes, I am. I think I will go and change first,' replied Tiana.

'Do you want me to come with you?' asked Leila.

'No thanks, it is okay. I'll be fine.'

'Fine, then we'll see you in the next class,' said Aliya.

Tiana got up to leave the hall. As she made her way through the messy maze of tables, she noticed that all eyes were on her. Some of them were even pointing in her direction and snickering openly.

Someday she thought, someday these pathologically twisted twits will learn some manners but then again, that may never happen. She got out of the hall and headed straight to the dorms. Her sweater was feeling itchy against her skin because it was completely drenched with water. She could not remove it because it was chilly. Even if she did, it wouldn't make much of a difference as a water-clogged sweater wasn't much of a help either.

After changing into dry clothes, she sat down on her bed to catch a minute of silence with herself. Before she knew it, she started to cry. She was shocked and surprised at herself for she was crying for such a silly reason. This was not half as bad as what had happened on the first day when everyone thought that she was a back-stabbing friend who stole boyfriends. She had not cried then, so why was she crying now?

'What's wrong with me?' wondered Tiana, wiping her tears.

She had been sitting on her bed for about ten minutes when her matron came into the dorms.

'What are you still doing here?' she asked curtly.

'Nothing ma'am. I was just about to leave,' said Tiana.

'You have already changed, so what are you waiting for?'

What's wrong with teachers? Can't they ever be polite?

'Yes ma'am, I am going.'

She left the dorms and went back to her class. By the time she entered, the class was mid-way through. The moment she entered, everyone started whispering and asking her questions.

'Tiana are you okay?' asked Aryan.

'Yes.'

'Did you go to the hospital?' asked Aliya.

'No.'

'But you should go,' insisted Bella.

'Fine.'

'You are so lucky. You have missed the entire physics class,' said Leila.

'Good.' Tiana sat down next to Leila.

'Stop that!' said Leila.

'What?' asked Tiana, raising her eyebrows.

'This talking in one word. Please, stop it. It's creepy,' said Leila.

'Sorry.'

'Again!' exclaimed Leila.

'What else do I say Leila? I have just become the biggest joke in school. I am upset and my head is hurting and just please don't ask me anything else. Okay?' Tiana's voice was cranky to the core.

'Relax. It's okay. So what if you fell in the dining hall. It does not matter, T.' Leila was trying her best to console her.

'It does matter to me. Everyone is having a hearty laugh at my expense,' groaned Tiana.

'What is wrong with you Tiana? Just yesterday you went and told Jasmine that it was okay. You gave her advice which you've failed to follow for yourself. That's called setting a real good example!' Leila's comment hit Tiana just where it was supposed to.

Leila was so right! Tiana realised that she was acting like a baby. And to think of it, she actually thought that she was strong. Here she was, crying about spilling water upon herself and well, also for falling off her chair in front of the entire school, but hey! Big deal! One should not fret about it forever.

'Hey, you're right Leila. I am just making a big deal out of nothing,' said Tiana apologetically, because she had lost her temper with Leila when Leila was just trying to help her practice what she preached.

'Chill! It's okay. I know it is a drag but never mind. Just try to forget about it, will ya? Everything will be alright,' consoled Leila.

Tiana's head was throbbing with pain now. It was as if a hundred men were hammering away at the back of her head. She still hadn't been to the hospital and now she regretted not going. Sitting in the class was just making her head hurt more and the big bump at the back of her head just felt bigger. Finally, the bell rang and they went outside for their break. Whenever Tiana crossed a group of people, they pointed at her and then burst out laughing. Yeah, now I can really forget about whatever had happened, she thought gloomily.

'It is so annoying. All these people are pointing at me and making fun of me. I hate this.'

'Just ignore them Tiana. Remember what we talked about,' reminded Leila.

'Yeah, it is so easy to give advice and really difficult to actually follow it,' said Tiana. 'But I'll try and not think about it.'

'Good for you,' said Bella.

All of them were sitting at the benches near the dining hall, the place where they usually spent time during their break between classes. Just then, Tiana's younger cousin brothers, Dhruv and Daksh, who had joined school in class five this year, came up to her.

'Hi guys! What are you dudes doing here?' asked Tiana, surprised to see her brothers.

'We just came to ask you if it is true that you fell off your chair in the dining hall,' asked Daksh. His question was followed by a roar of laughter.

'And that you spilled water on yourself?' chimed Dhruv.

How was she supposed to forget about it for God's sake?

'Who told you about it?' asked Bella.

'Everyone is talking about it and making fun of Tia,' said Daksh, as if it was the most natural thing for everyone to make fun of their cousin sister.

'Yes. Okay, it's true. All that you have heard. So just stop talking about it,' said Tiana, sounding as cranky as ever.

'So you really fell off the chair?' asked Dhruv.

'Yes.'

'And dropped water on yourself?' asked Daksh, laughing away.

'Yes,' said Tiana in a bored voice.

'And that you got detention for not finishing prep on time?'
'Hey wait a minute. Who told you about that?' asked Leila.
'Our friends,' said Daksh.
'The news spreads like forest fire here,' said Savera.
'Yes, even that's true. So?' Tiana was feeling resigned now.
'So nothing so. It is just a very bad day for you. And we are fighting with anyone who makes fun of you,' said Daksh.
'What?' exclaimed Tiana shocked and touched at the same time. Her crankiness was instantly placated.
'We said that we are . . .'
'No, I got what you said. Thanks guys but please, no more fighting. Promise?' asked Tiana.
'Why, we like to fight,' protested Dhruv.
'But I don't. Please, no more fighting for me,' said Tiana firmly.
'We thought you would be happy to know that we were fighting for you,' said Daksh. He seemed disappointed.
'Thank you. This is very sweet. It really is. But I don't want you to fight for me. Fighting does not help. Please. You just promise me that you will stop. Will you?' said Tiana desperately.
'Your sister is right,' said Leila, trying to help.
After some more rounds of convincing by the girls, they agreed to stop.
'So you take care of yourselves . . . and write letters to your mom,' said Tiana, donning the role of an elder sister and playing it to perfection.
'Okay. Bye Tia!' said Daksh, and they went back to their class.
'That was so cute T. They are adorable,' said Savera.
'They were actually fighting with whoever made fun of you,' laughed Celia.
'Yeah,' said Tiana, unable to control her smile any more.
'That's a lot of fights,' said Leila.
'I know!' laughed Tiana. And somehow, laughing made her feel better. Or maybe it was the effect of the painkiller that the

nurse had given her for her head. The bell rang announcing the end of their break.

Tiana had finally managed to finish her prep in time. So that was one thing off her long list of things to be taken care of. After the never-ending Bio class (which was their last class), the day in school drew its end. All of them rushed off to eat lunch.

When Tiana sat down on her chair, the morning's horrible incident came rushing back to her. To add to the wonderful recall, some of the guys from her class came up to her and asked her to sit tight on her seat.

Tiana gave them a livid glare. It must have translated as – I'll bite off your heads if you dare to utter another word. The guys immediately took an about turn and hurried away instead of answering back.

Good, thought Tiana.

'Well done pal! You scared the hell out of them. Like Veer,' said Bella bitterly.

'They deserved it. And so did Veer,' shrugged Tiana.

'Absolutely,' agreed Bella.

After that, no one really made fun of Tiana and the rest of the day was pretty boring compared to the morning.

However, that night was a nightmare.

During dinner, the lights went off. It was completely dark inside the dining hall. And absolute darkness gives both the notorious girls and boys a perfect reason to start a food fight. So the moment the lights went off, salad, water and vegetables were flying in every direction! This was not the first food fight that Tiana had witnessed. So she knew what she had to do, and that was to duck under the table till the lights came back on. This time though, she was a little late in saving herself. Just when she was about to hide, someone poured some thick hot liquid thing all over her hair, face and shoulders. She was shocked into the mouth-wide-open mode. There was no chance to even find out who did it because of the darkness. Then she realised that the liquid was not just any liquid... it was daal. Daal! Oh God! She was soaked in yellow daal! It was slithering down her shampooed hair, clean face and marching its way to her till now dry sweater. Oh!

What a !@#$%^&*! PERFECT END TO A PERFECT DAY!!! Just then, the lights came back on. Everyone was squinting their eyes because of the sudden light after total darkness. When they noticed what had happened to Tiana, everyone started howling with laughter. This attracted attention from the other tables as well and soon, everyone was pointing at Tiana's yellow hair and face. They kept on roaring with laughter. Tiana was sitting in her chair fuming with rage. Luckily, Leila's lecture in the morning came to her rescue. Don't make a big deal. It is okay.

That's when Tiana decided to follow her own advice. Wasn't she the one who hated self-pity? That was what she had been doing for the entire day and she was feeling sorry for herself even right now. After looking at all her friends laugh like maniacs, she realised that she must be looking very funny after all. Why sit and feel her blood boil when she could laugh it off? So what if it was embarrassing? One should not spoil one's mood over it. Besides, this was a once in a lifetime kind of an experience. After all, how many times was an entire bowl of daal poured over your head? So many people have gone through life without that experience! So, when all her friends were rolling about with laughter, she joined them. It is pretty easy to laugh at yourself once you have the courage to do so.

When Bella and Leila finally noticed that even Tiana was laughing with them, they stopped laughing. Tiana felt good when she saw the expression on their faces. She showed a change. She liked this change. Especially now, since her quest had started... which reminded her that this was another answer for her 'finding it' questions. These two incidents just had to be her most embarrassing moments. No doubts about it. They would be for anyone.

'Tia, are you okay? I mean, I don't know what to say,' said Leila.

'I am really sorry for laughing like this but it is so hilarious and . . . ' Bella didn't want to finish the sentence so Tiana did the honours.

'It is very funny, I get it too,' said Tiana.

'You do get it?' asked Leila surprised.

'Yes I actually do. At least you are saved from eating the daal,' giggled Tiana.

'How come you're not seething with rage right now? That's weird. I thought you would be angry. But you're laughing . . . and that too at yourself,' said Leila slowly.

'In fact, I am enjoying laughing at myself and I am also enjoying all the attention,' laughed Tiana.

'How come?' repeated a perplexed Leila.

'Thanks to you,' said Tiana.

'How did I help? Oh! What I said in the morning? You actually decided to follow it?' said Leila, amazed at her own ability to influence this tough nut.

'Yes I did. Shouldn't I have done so?' asked Tiana.

'Of course you should have. I am so glad I helped,' said Leila happily, 'It is so great that you decided to see it this way. Isn't it easy?'

'Actually it really is easy,' chirped Tiana.

'You know I would have hugged you if not for that . . . ,' Leila pointed at the daal dripping from her head and sweater.

'Oh, yes of course I know,' said Tiana, nodding her head.

'Do you want some tissues?' asked Bella, laughing alongside.

'Yes but I think I'll need lots of them,' laughed Tiana.

But she still took some tissues from Bella and wiped her face. She didn't want a fat ugly zit on her nose, forehead, chin or any other part of her face first thing in the morning.

'Today just hasn't been your day, huh?' asked Bella.

'Oh, but from where I see it, it has been just my day. Everyone has been talking about me. I have embarrassed myself into the next century and I learnt a very important thing – I learnt to laugh at myself. So I am happy!'

Tiana believed that her friends were the epitome of cool. They were absolutely in sync with the latest stuff in fashion and trends. The girls were worthy of leading the French fashion industry and the boys were always seen with the latest, most expensive and weirdest gadgets. Even the boys were hooked on to the latest fads in fashion. With their spunky hair styles and trendy accessories, they have started giving competition to the girls! Looking good was of utmost importance to them as well. Tiana thought that boys are a billion times more brand conscious than girls. Brands had become an obsession. Girls would wear whatever they liked but the guys had gone crazy! In junior classes, this brand phenomenon was under control but as they grew older there came a time when all they talked about was BRANDS. They wanted to know who was wearing which brand when they were not in school (thanks to uniforms!). They went out of their way to prove that what they were wearing was better than what some other guys were wearing. Their watches had to be Mont Blanc or Rolex, perfumes had to be Paco Rabanne, jeans had to be Calvin Klein, boxers had to be Tommy Hilfiger and bathroom slippers had to be Nike or Adidas! Bathroom slippers!

Initially, it was just a handful of people who were under the brand spell. But these very few were highly successful in sucking everyone into the brand cult. So much so that these guys started gifting expensive gadgets like PSPs and cell phones to each other for their birthdays! Come on, get real. And this trend sure seems like it's here to stay. It's not going anywhere. She didn't support it but she could not do anything about it either. She felt sorry for those who could not afford all these uselessly lavish things because they were getting huge complexes from those who could afford all this. It wasn't fair considering the fact that parents were the ones who were paying for all this. It's as if parents aren't doing enough already. But just like in the case of drinking, her pleas for controlling their expensive urges fell on deaf ears.

She loved her friends . . . there was no doubt about it. But that did not mean that she understood everything about them either. They were quite complex to figure out. A lot of their decisions confused her. For example, Tiana could never understand why they continued doing something they didn't even like in the first place. Take for instance, her best friend Leila. Tiana knew that Leila and Bella hated drinking. They told her so themselves. But in spite of that, they continued drinking. She had asked them a hundred times the reason why they persisted upon this stupid course of action and each time she got the same reply. A reply she didn't understand at all. This is how the very first conversation sounded. And it sounded the same ever since.

Tiana: Didn't you tell me yourself that you hate to drink?
Bella: Yeah, so?
Tiana: So? You are drinking.
Leila: Relax Tiana. We are not addicted. It's not like we are depsos or something.
Tiana: So why are you drinking?
Bella: How many times do we have to tell you?
Leila: We are social drinkers.
Tiana: Come on, if you continue like this I will soon have to remove the social. And I would hate to do that.
Leila: It's okay. It's cool to drink you know.
Tiana: No, I don't know. Who said so?
Bella: See, all our boyfriends drink. And we go out together and it sounds very weird if we ask for Coke. You know what I mean?
Tiana: I really don't know what you mean Bella. All I can make out is that you are ashamed of yourself.
Bella: I am not!
Tiana: Why else would you feel weird asking for Coke? Coke is your real choice, but since it is not good enough for some

people, you forget your own self to seem cool . . . which proves that you are ashamed of yourself and your choices.
Bella: Whatever!
Leila: Tiana, it is not such a big deal.

She had stopped after that. Clearly, her pleas were falling on deaf ears. One thing Tiana was completely against was drinking . . . especially underage drinking. She simply abhorred smoking. She had tried her best to stop all her friends from drinking but had failed miserably. Under their boyfriends' influence, they had become 'social drinkers'. As far as Tiana was concerned, there is nothing known as a social drinker. Once you get addicted to that vice, you're trapped for good and there is just no turning back. Why were her friends trying to grow up so fast? Why didn't they have the integrity to be proud of themselves and their choices?

These days, she felt that they needed to start 'finding it' more than her. Her friends had started drinking and then smoking in front of Tiana's very own eyes. They never had the good sense to think that it could harm them or that their bodies are not ready for it. They thought that they were invincible . . . that nothing in the world could harm them. They just wanted to go ahead and experiment with it because it was considered cool and made them feel important. Besides, everyone was doing it. They thought that it was an important part of growing up. Phuhlease! Wait people! You have entire an lifetime to feel important. Just wait a bit.

Of course, no one listened to her.

But she never stopped trying. At least when she was around, they hardly drank. Who knew what they were doing behind her back. Maybe they were drinking even more.

If only girls her age respected themselves and learnt to stand up against something they thought was wrong instead of going with the flow and doing what everyone did. IF only. Teenage girls needed to be more careful than boys about things like drinking because teen girls have a greater risk of damaging their brains than the males. It was true. It messed up the brain functions which led to

Veer had finally started attending classes and when he noticed that Bella was already dating someone else, and that there was no chance of them being together again, he decided to go for some other girl too.

Unfortunately the other girl he chose to date turned out to be Tiana again. Two days after being discharged from the hospital, Veer came up to her when she was alone in the classroom.

'Hi Tiana!' Veer had said.

Tiana had been reading a book. She looked up and saw the creep standing right in front of her.

'Yeah whatever!' Tiana had replied coolly and started reading again.

'I got discharged,' Veer had continued, trying hard to get her attention.

'Whatever!' This time she didn't even look up.

'At least look at me Tia,' persisted Veer.

Tiana saw red! Her blood started boiling again and her temper levels were just about to reach the danger mark! If he was not careful enough this time she was sure she would break his nose.

'Tia, I am trying to be nice okay,' he went on.

That's it. That did it.

'How dare you talk to me? How dare you call me Tia? How dare you have the guts to even come in front of me and say that you are trying to be nice, you filthy moron!'

'Hey, relax. So I acted like a jerk but come on, you can't drag that forever Tia.' Veer was talking as if he was doing her a favour by asking her out again. His tone also assumed Tia to be his best friend. He was not getting the clue that if he continued like this he would soon be in the hospital again.

'Don't you dare call me Tia. Don't you dare!' Tiana was screaming at the top of her voice. She sounded and looked dangerous.

'Why not?'

'Because I hate, loathe, despise and can't stand you! Get it?' Tiana had replied with all the bitterness she could muster.

'Come on Tiana. Stop pretending. You like me. I know you do.' Veer was completely sure of himself. He was in every possible way a self-obsessed sicko!

Tiana blinked. Several times. Did he just say what she thought he said? Is that what Veer thought? That she liked him? From where did that thought come into his pea brain? God! What had she done to deserve this?

'Excuse me?' she had asked blankly, just to be sure that she had heard correctly.

'You heard me. I know you like me. So stop pretending and we could start going out Tia. Last time you refused because I was still dating Bella but now thanks to you, Bella is dating someone else. Problem solved.' Veer had smiled complacently, smug in his own opinion of his mirror cracking material looks.

'Is this some kind of joke? Or have you completely lost your mind. And how did I help in making Bella date someone else?' Tiana had asked, amused that he actually thought that she would agree to date him. He is sooooo dumb!

'You planned it yourself,' Veer had replied.

'Oh, really? I planned it? How so?'

'You told Bella the truth and then obviously she broke up with me and started dating some senior, and now we are both free to date. I lost my girlfriend because of you, so this is the least you can do for me, right?' Veer had said this very seriously.

Was this guy for real? The audacity to think that she did all this because she liked him! The least she could do for him because he had lost his girlfriend because of her! Oh yeah? But she really didn't want to waste any more of her time with him.

'Get out,' Tiana had said calmly, trying hard not to lose her temper.

'Tia, stop acting.'

'DON'T YOU CALL ME TIA!' She had screamed so loudly that all her friends standing outside the class rushed in to see what had happened.

'Tiana, are you okay?' Aliya had asked. 'We heard you scream.'

'Very loudly.'

'What's wrong?'

'And what is he doing here?' Celia had asked, pointing at Veer.

'He thinks that I like him. And he is asking me out.' Tiana glared at Veer who looked taken aback at how things were going. Apparently, he was under the impression that Tiana would jump at the thought of going out with him. Which world was he living in?

'What?' Leila had cried out.

'He thinks that?' Celia had said.

'Veer, do you really think that Tiana likes you?' Aliya had asked, looking squarely at Veer. He didn't say anything at all.

'What are you, nuts?' Celia had asked.

'Tia, he actually asked you out?' Leila had asked her, amazed at the foolishness of this dim-wit.

'Not just that. He says it is the least I can do as he lost his girlfriend because of me!'

'What? How did this happen because of you?' Lilly had asked.

'He thinks that I have been planning this entire thing so that I could go out with him. He thinks I told Bella everything,' Tiana had explained.

'This is the weirdest thing I have ever heard,' Savera had said, tapping her head.

'I swear!' agreed Leila.

'Veer, Tiana didn't tell Bella anything,' chipped in Aliya.

'Karam told all of us okay,' added Leila.

'So keep your disgusting theories to yourselves,' said Savera.

All of them were staring at him in sheer disbelief.

'And leave her alone,' said Bella.

It was the first time Bella had spoken during this entire fiasco. She had been standing quietly all this while behind Veer. He turned to look at her.

'Bella, I am so sorry,' Veer had said, staring at his shoes.

For a moment, Bella just looked at him as if he was some object of great interest. Then she shifted her gaze to Tiana, looked at Veer again and then slapped him real hard. All of them were shocked. Veer didn't even know what hit him! He was startled out of his meagre senses! By now, a lot of people had come inside the class and Veer looked visibly humiliated. There were a lot of people standing outside the class as well. Everyone had seen Bella slap him and now, they were laughing and jeering at the scooting Veer. He had no choice but to rush out of the class.

'Wow! Bella that was great!' Lilly couldn't find a word to describe it.

'That was amazing!' exclaimed Tiana.

'It felt amazing too!' Bella felt triumphant.

'I am sure it did. He deserved it,' said Aliya.

That day Bella slapping Veer was the only thing that was discussed in school. It was the hot topic in school.

The only spoiler was that the senior mistress found out about it too and called Bella to her office. She lectured Bella about 'appropriate ladylike behaviour' and reminded Bella that she was a girl and that slapping a fellow student is not acceptable for a well mannered girl. Blah blah blah! Basically, Bella had to listen to gibberish for thirty minutes and by the end of it she got detention on Sunday again.

By now, everyone had forgotten about the daal incident too . . . mainly because something bigger had happened – a guy had been caught with alcohol in school and his parents had been called up to come and take him away. A boy getting expelled is bigger news than a food fight. But the worst thing was that this story got published in a local newspaper and now, everyone outside the school knew about it too. It is hard because most people seem to think that all the kids in boarding schools are spoilt brats and that doing drugs and taking alcohol is like second nature to them.

Whenever any one found out that Tiana is in a boarding school she was asked about this drugs-alcohol thing from parents who thought that keeping their children with them in the same house meant that everything was in control. But they were wrong . . . so wrong.

This theory is not fool-proof. Don't they see that kids in normal schools have so much more access to all these things than the ones in boarding schools who are constantly surrounded by teachers throughout the day and night? In boarding schools, students hardly have any interaction with the outside world. If even five per cent of them get into drinking and drugs, ninety five per cent of them are clean! Much more than the normal schools!

But when people (especially parents) have a mental block against boarding schools, then no matter what you say to them, they will just not understand your point of view. Tiana had already thrown up her hands in acceptance of her inability to convince such parents . . . she didn't bother to even try now.

∽

Tiana found it very amusing that even though she was in a boarding school where things could get really monotonous and boring, it was actually just the opposite. So many things kept happening around her. The most recent one had actually shocked her more than amused her.

She and her friends had just found out that their senior mistress hated them. This was not some childish rant against their teacher. She really hated them. They knew this for sure now because the senior mistress called them bitches! Oh yeah! A woman at such a senior position in such a good school and she was verbally abusing the students! Their fault was that Bella, Leila and Lilly were making fun of some girls who were currently at logger heads with Bella and Leila. The senior mistress found that out. She then called all of them to her office. But instead of correcting them she started saying all kinds of weird things like:-

'You girls are absolute inhuman bitches. Always picking on other girls and making fun of teachers. If I had to spend a day with you all in a room you would stone me to death too! You all are just frustrated. The girls from your own batch don't like you. The boys from your batch don't like you. Juniors, seniors and teachers . . . nobody in this school likes you. You are all a pain for everyone.'

She went on screaming on top of her lungs for fifteen minutes. The girls actually thought that she was just saying whatever she had heard about herself! Everyone in the school called her frustrated. Nobody seemed to like her . . . not even the teachers. No one can help it . . . she is just too nosy and mean! Who knew that teasing some girls who are fighting with you could become such a big deal? But they should have known better, because the girls they were fighting with were not only the 'other' gang of their class but they also happened to be senior mistress' favourites.

But just imagine, how could a teacher say stuff like this to the students? Talk about her manners and ladylike behaviour! On top of that, she gave all of them a physical drill! That means they would have to get up at five in the morning and do some sort of physical activity which will kill them with pain and give them nasty cramps for a week.

'I am so sorry guys. You people didn't even do anything and now you have been punished because of me,' apologised Bella.

'It's okay girl! She would have found some other way of punishing us anyway. Chill out,' said Aliya.

'Come on, let's finish our prep. We can't stay up late tonight if we have to get up at 5 am,' said Tiana.

The mug-it-up fever was still riding high, even though they would appear for the Boards next year. Tiana didn't even want to think about what would happen when the exams would be only a month away. Today, a really hilarious incident happened with her. Tiana's class was supposed to have an English class at 11.30 am but their teacher was not feeling well so she was not teaching them. Everyone decided to make good use of their free time and started playing Truth and Dare instead. (This was Leila's idea.) But Tiana had opted out. She was quietly sitting on her seat and reading her book when suddenly she heard Jai (Leila's ex) call her name. She looked up from her book and saw that he was kneeling in front of her.

'What the hell are you doing Jai?' asked Tiana, puzzled.

'Tiana, you are a bird and I am your feathers,' said Jai spreading his arms.

'What?' asked Tiana, baffled. Then she looked up and saw that the entire class was staring at her. That's when she realised what was happening. It was one of Leila's stupid ideas for dares.

'Ha ha! Very funny Leila,' laughed Tiana.

Everyone burst out laughing.

'You figured out that it was a dare. How come?' asked Leila.

'By the way you all were staring at me and because no normal person says stuff like this to anyone,' said Tiana simply.

'Oh no! I told you guys not to make it so obvious,' said Bella, giggling in between.

'Better luck next time,' said Tiana.

Jai was on his feet again when Leila asked him to finish the dare.

'What's the point? Tiana knows that it is a dare now,' said Jai.

'So what? Finish it now,' urged Leila.

So he got down on his knees and spread his arms again.

'God! This is so gross! Please, stop it! You don't need to do this. Get up,' said Tiana.

'No you do. Hurry up Jai,' said Leila.

'Tiana, I am not just your feather, you are . . .'

Tiana didn't hear exactly what she was because just then their teacher came into the class and saw what was happening.

'That is just so beautiful Jai. All you need is a ring and then you can propose to her properly,' said their teacher, visibly irritated.

This comment made everyone laugh. Even Tiana. Only Jai seemed to be blushing like a boiled beetroot.

Tiana knew that once they left school, these little incidents would always come back to her as fond memories. She would miss these days of fun. Whatever kind of weirdoes her friends might be, she couldn't have asked for more. They were the best.

Tiana was very happy with the way her 'finding it' quest was going on too. It had really made a huge difference to her life . . . like she had hoped.

It felt so good. She discovered things which she had never known about herself. She was doing things she had never done before—she could laugh at herself, she had stopped taking things too seriously and she did not feel the need to justify herself for everything she did or said. It made her feel cheerful and relaxed. It felt good because she felt in control of her life. Finally!

During lunch everyone was talking about the dare.

'You should have seen the expression on Tiana's face when Jai knelt down and called her a bird,' Bella was telling Rehan.

'You really looked shocked Tia,' laughed Leila.

'Why am I the centre of all your dares? Why?' grumbled Tiana.

'Because yours are the best reactions. And thanks to your quest these days, you do the most unexpected of things,' replied Leila.

'Wow! Thanks a lot!' smiled Tiana.

'You are always welcome!' Leila smiled back.

'By the way, what had you asked Jai to say to me?' asked Tiana.

'After the bird thing we asked him to say that you are honey and he is a bee and that you are a cake and he is the icing,' laughed Leila.

'You what? I don't believe this! From where do you get these weird ideas Leila? Honey and bee! Cake and icing! Are you crazy?' asked Tiana.

'Call me crazy but it is funny,' said Leila honestly.

'That's true,' agreed Tiana, smiling at her best friend.

Just then Karam came up to their table.

'Leila, mom and dad have come,' said Karam, carefully avoiding Tiana's eyes.

'What? Mom and dad are here in school? Why? What are they doing here?' asked Leila, startled.

'I don't know. I was just told that they are in the school office and they have called us over there. That's it. Did you do something wrong?' asked Karam suspiciously.

'No I have done nothing,' said Leila defensively. And then, as if not sure of her own self, she wanted a confirmation from someone else too. 'Actually, I don't know. Tiana did I do something wrong?'

'I can't think of anything. No,' replied Tiana. Even she was surprised at this news.

'Let's go. We need to go to the school office immediately,' said Karam.

'I will see you later,' said Leila and she got up to leave.

'Okay. Bye and best of luck!' said Tiana.

'Thanks!'

They left. Things were not improving with Karam. In fact, if anything, they had become worse. Karam always said hi to her. This time, he had not even looked in her direction. This is what she gets for trying not to make things awkward between them. She had lost a good friend for good. She still hadn't told Leila anything about it. Maybe she should.

But what was annoying Tiana the most was the fact that she was missing talking to Karam. Why? She didn't like him any more than a friend, but he was interesting to talk to. He was the only guy with whom she could have decent sensible conversations. He had always helped her and used to tell her that everything would be fine when she messed things up. But he didn't say that things would be fine when daal had been poured over her head or when she had fallen off her chair. He hadn't made fun of Veer when Veer had asked her out. Nothing. Karam was just not talking to her anymore. This bothered her. But why? He is just a friend, right? But then she thought about her 'finding it' mission. Wasn't she supposed to find honest answers and her true feelings? Honestly, she was starting to realise that after all this, maybe she did like Karam . . . a lot more than just as a friend.

∽

When Tiana opened her eyes, she was back in her bed. It was not dark any more. Sid had switched on all the lights. Light–it made her feel better. Her mom was sitting on a chair next to her bed. When she noticed that Tiana was awake, she leaned forward.

'How are you darling?' asked her mother.

Tiana tried to sit up but could do so with a lot difficulty. It took a lot of energy. Her mom helped her prop up on the bed.

'Tia, you are very weak and the doctor has asked me to make you eat something. If not eat, then at least drink something,' said her mother. *She looked worried and concerned.*

'I can't,' said Tiana. *Her voice sounded hoarse.*

'I know. It is tough. I know, Tia. But please listen to me,' *pleaded her mother.*

Tiana nodded her head and her mother went out of the room to get her something to eat. As soon as she left, her dad, Sid and her cousin brothers, Dhruv and Daksh, came into her room (they had come to stay with their aunt during the holidays).

'Tia, how are you feeling now?' asked her dad.

'Not good dad. Not good at all,' replied Tiana slowly.
'It's okay. It will be fine,' said Sid.
'I hope so,' said Tiana.
Her mother came into the room with a bowl of piping hot soup.
'Here, drink this slowly,' she said.
'Thanks.'
'Tiana, we just want to tell you that your mom, brothers and I are proud of you. You made the correct decision you know,' said her dad.
'Thanks dad,' said Tiana.
'Some officers want to talk to you. All the parents want to know what exactly happened and you are the only one who saw it happen. Only you can clear their doubts,' said Sid.
'They have been waiting to talk to you for the entire day. Are you ready to do this? The sooner the better honey,' said her mom.
No, she was not ready for this. This meant that she would have to relive the horrible incident once again . . . those few minutes when she was all alone with the wrecked car in front of her and she hadn't known what to do . . . when she thought that she was about to lose her friends. No way . . . that's the last thing she would want to do, but she had no choice.
'Fine. The sooner the better,' said Tiana and suddenly, before she knew it, she burst out crying. It was as if she had no control over them. She just had to vent out the frustration and sorrow that was raging within her.
'Tia please don't cry.' Her mother hugged her tightly.
'You don't have to talk to them today,' said Sid.
'No I need to. I just want to finish off with this today itself,' sobbed Tiana.
'Are you sure?' asked her mom.
'Yes, I am,' said Tiana, wiping away her tears.
'Fine. I will give them a call then. But you had better finish that soup,' smiled her mother. Then her mom and dad left the room.
The twins were looking very nervous.
'Tiana please don't cry,' said Daksh.
'Sid says that you are very weak. You do want chocolate don't you?' asked Dhruv.

Tiana smiled weakly at her brothers.

'Yes I would love to have some chocolate.'

They looked very excited at the idea of helping Tiana. They rushed out to get chocolate for her. At the same time, her mother came in again.

'Tia, they will be here in half-an-hour to talk to you,' she said.

FIVE

The fact that she liked Karam a lot more than a friend made her squirm in her tummy. It was a weird uncomfortable feeling. Now what? She would have to tell Leila about it but what will she say to Karam? He had asked her out twice and both the times she had refused. Now what could she say to him? That she had just changed her mind suddenly. Uff! How lame! She felt like she was a big time loser in this case.

Tiana was walking back to the dorms thinking about her useless situation. As she was lost in thoughts, she didn't notice a pot hole in front of her and stepped right into it.

'Tia, what's wrong with you?' asked Bella, staring disgustingly at Tiana's wet and muddy shoes and stockings.

'I don't know,' muttered Tiana, feeling stupid.

'What were you thinking about?' asked Savera.

'Me? Oh yes, about why Leila's parents have come,' lied Tiana.

'Oh yes, that was like a big surprise for Leila,' said Lilly.

'I know. She was convinced that she had done something wrong,' said Bella.

'But I'm sure she didn't do anything,' stated Savera.

Tiana was glad that the conversation had moved on from her. But she was curious to know why Leila's parents had come to their school. She hoped that everything was fine. Leila was still in the school office with Karam, so she would have to wait to find out the reason for this visit.

Tiana had just reached the dorms and was removing her wet shoes and socks when a junior girl came and gave her a letter. It was from Sid. She opened it.

Hi Tiana,
Life is very boring without you guys. I really miss school. How is Leila? And the twins? I hope they are not causing too much trouble. Anyway, my launch party is in two weeks and you all will be here by then. I am really looking forward to seeing you. And Tiana, I know it might sound a little awkward coming from me but Karam is a great guy and he likes you a lot. I have known this for quite some time now but he asked me not to tell you or anyone else. He told me that he was going to ask you out before the Kick Off. So did everything go well with him? I hope it did. I won't mention this to you again because I know it's very embarrassing . . . for me too. So you take care and study hard. You are in class ten after all. Mom and dad are fine. They want you to take care of the twins. Bye and see you soon.
Sid

Tiana just stared at the letter after she read it. She read the part about Karam again, blinked several times and re-read it. Sid knew! Her big brother really knew her big secret . . . as it has turned out . . . it was never really a secret. Why did Karam tell Sid? Why? This just sucks. Oh God! Her life was becoming a bigger mess everyday. She had better tell Leila about all this before Sid or Karam blabbered something to her. But Leila didn't return till five in the evening. When she did come, she told Tiana something which messed up her life even more.

'Wh . . . what?' stammered Tiana, 'You're kidding right?'
    'Its true,' said Leila.

'But why, how, when?' asked Tiana, baffled beyond words.
'That's why mom and dad came up to school,' said Leila.
'Oh hellllllll!' exclaimed Tiana.
'I was shocked when mom told us about it,' said Leila.
'So are you really going to . . . to huh?' asked Tiana in disbelief.
'Yes, I am moving to Paris,' said Leila.

That's right. Leila and her family were moving to Paris. Her mom and dad had gone to Paris after all of them had come to school and they really liked it over there. Her dad, on impulse, decided to move to Paris. He had already tied up a contract with Le Soir. The company was only too eager to have an award winning photographer on their rolls.

On impulse! Who moves to a new country on impulse? Nobody except for Leila's dad, who had already bought a house there. But that's not the point. The point was that Leila would be leaving school. Hey, not only was she leaving the school, she was also leaving the city and the country. Leila, her best friend . . . her unofficial shrink . . . the only person who helped her retain her sanity throughout these messy times caused by factors ranging from the Boards to boys. And talking about boys reminded her that Karam would be moving away too. For the first time she genuinely liked a boy and whoosh! He is moving to Paris. Not that the situation with Karam was anything but hopeless. But now, it was just impossible.

But Leila was going to Paris. Tiana was still trying to recover from the shock.

'When are you going?' asked Tiana.
'Very soon actually. After the break,' replied Leila.
'What? That is like less than two weeks!' said Tiana, stunned.

'I know everything is happening so fast. Mom and dad came today to withdraw us from the school. We won't return to school after the break. I don't know how I feel about this entire thing, it is so unreal,' said Leila.

'Withdraw you? They came to withdraw you! So it is really happening, huh? There is no turning back,' sighed Tiana.

'There is no turning back. Mom has already started packing the stuff in the house and getting rid of the extra furniture. She just has two weeks left for all this,' said Leila.

'How do you feel about this?' asked Tiana.

'I am still not sure. I mean my entire life is here. All of you, Sid and the school. I didn't know that when I wished to go to Paris, I would actually shift there,' said Leila thoughtfully.

'Be careful about what you wish for,' said Tiana dimly.

'I swear it,' smiled Leila.

'But you want to go, right?' asked Tiana. She wanted to know what Leila wanted.

'Yes, I kinda do want to go. It's a whole new world waiting for me out there. I just think it will be a great new experience for me and my family, you know what I mean?' asked Leila, desperately wanting Tiana to understand her situation.

'Of course I understand Leila. I do. It will be great for you. I mean, it is PARIS. After all, even I want to go there. Maybe not live there but I know that it's a beautiful city. Plus there are always all those romantic type French guys,' trailed off Tiana.

'Oh please! Come on, I still like your brother,' said Leila.

Brother. This reminded Tiana about Karam again. She had to tell Leila and now was the best time.

'Leila . . . firstly, I got a letter from Sid today,' said Tiana.

'Really? What did it say?' asked Leila.

'That his launch party is during our break and we will be with him. Wait a minute, you will be there right?' asked Tiana.

'Yes, of course I will be there. I told mom and dad that this would be the last time that I would get to spend time with you all. We will be leaving after that,' said Leila.

'Thank God you will be there! It's Sid's big night after all,' said Tiana.

'Tia, I will really miss you,' sighed Leila.

'I will miss you too,' replied Tiana.

They hugged each other but they did NOT cry.

'I have to tell you something else as well,' said Tiana, a little uneasily.

'Sure, what do you want to tell me?' asked Leila.

'It is about your brother,' said Tiana.

'Well, what about him?' asked Leila, leaning forward with a question mark on her face.

'Karam asked me out before the Kick Off . . . then again during the Kick Off. I refused both the times. He said that he likes me. Sid already knew about the entire thing. He has known about it for quite some time now, at least that's what I can make out from his letter,' said Tiana quickly.

Leila took her time to digest this piece of information.

'My brother likes you?'

'Yes.'

'My brother Karam?'

'How many brothers do you have?' asked Tiana. She could not make out anything from Leila's expression.

'And he asked you out? Twice?'

'Yes.'

Till now Leila's face was completely blank, but as soon as the news finally managed to HIT her, she suddenly let out a shrill cry.

'Eww! That's just so eww! And weird. I mean, he is my brother and you are my b . . . best friend,' stuttered Leila.

'At least now you know how I felt when you started going out with Sid,' said Tiana, satisfied that Leila finally understood the weird feeling.

'So that's how you felt? I am so sorry Tia! I never really tried to understand why you didn't want me and Sid to be together,' reflected Leila.

'Finally Leila, finally you get it,' said Tiana happily.

'So Karam just came up to you and asked you out?' asked Leila.

'Yes, that is exactly what happened,' said Tiana, relieved to have finally shared the news with her best friend. Not telling Leila about it was like indigestion in the tummy . . . and that surely isn't a very pleasant feeling!

'You must have been shocked!'

'Of course I was. It was so unexpected. And Sid knew about it?' asked Leila, laughing.

'Can you imagine? I was stunned. Sid knew about it and gave me advice!' said Tiana.

'Oh God! This has been quite a day for me,' giggled Leila.

'For you AND me,' emphasised Tiana.

'I will miss talking to you like this,' said Leila.

'You'll always be my best friend,' smiled Tiana.

'And you will be mine,' Leila smiled back.

'Before you give my post to some French mademoiselle,' added Tiana with a wink.

'Shut up will ya? But I want to ask you something and you have to tell me the truth, okay?' said Leila.

'Ahemmmm,' said Tiana.

'Do you like Karam?' asked Leila.

Oh dear! Wrong question. How could she tell the truth to Leila? It would really mess up everything. And then, what if Karam found out? It would be so embarrassing for her! No can do. She would have to lie. She would not tell the truth at any cost.

'I am waiting T,' said Leila breaking into Tiana's conversation with herself.

'Yes, I do like him,' blurted out Tiana. The words just came out . . . it was as if she had no control over her mouth. Though for a moment, Tia felt like gobbling up her words, she knew that this was inevitable. She could not lie forever and now was a good time to 'fess up too.

'Oh no! Why? What do you see in him?' asked Leila in sheer disbelief.

'What do you see in Sid?' asked Tiana, turning the tables swiftly.

'Good point!' muttered Leila.

'Thank you!'

'So have you told him? Wait a sec. If you like Karam why did you refuse to go out with him? Twice?' asked Leila, looking like Sherlock Holmes on a mission.

'Because till then I was still in state of shock and didn't know that I liked him. And now that I don't get to talk to him, I have realised that I miss talking to him and that I like his company,' said Tiana, getting defensive.

'So do you want to go out with him?' asked Leila.

'Leila, you guys are moving to Paris in two weeks time. Get real. I can't date a guy who is moving to another continent.'

'But what if we weren't moving? Then would you go out with him?'

'Maybe. But you are moving so there is no point in the discussion.'

'That's true. But I guess Karam is better than Veer,' said Leila.

'Veer? When was he even a choice?' laughed Tiana.

'But really, that guy has the nerve to ask you out after all that he did,' said Leila.

'Veer is such a waste of time. I don't give a damn about him,' said Tiana, clicking her fingers to show her indifference.

Just then, Bella, Savera, Aliya, Lilly and Celia came into the dorm.

'Hi Leila! So you finally came back from the school office,' said Lilly.

'Hi guys!' replied Leila.

'So what were your parents doing here?' asked Bella.

'Did you do something wrong?' added Celia.

'No, I hadn't done anything,' said Leila.

'Thank God!' exclaimed Savera.

'But I have some news. Some big news,' said Leila, facing all of them.

'What? I hope everything is okay?' said Bella, sensing that something wasn't quite right.

'My family is shifting to Paris,' said Leila excitedly.

'That's great! So you will go there during your holidays. How lucky!' exclaimed Bella.

'No no no. All of us are shifting. My parents came to withdraw us from the school today. Karam and I will not return to school after the break,' explained Leila.

'What?' cried out Aliya.

'You are going for good? I don't believe this!' said Savera, shocked to hear this.

'Afraid so, yes,' said Leila.

'But this sucks. When will we see you again? I mean, Paris is awfully far off,' said Bella. Clearly, the news hadn't gone down very well with her gang of girls.

'How did this happen?' asked Celia.

Leila started telling them the entire story about her father and that he wanted to live in Paris. Tiana had already heard everything. She went back to her bed (she had been sitting on Leila's bed which would be empty in two weeks time) and fell on it face first. Then she thought about how much her life would change without her closest friend. She had been friends with Leila for four years now. She shared everything with her. She could confide in Leila because she trusted her.

And now she would be gone in three weeks after the launch party. She would really miss her. But we need to keep accepting changes in life. We need to evolve and keep up with the times and the changes that it brings. This was that time. That's when she got the idea of throwing a farewell party for Leila. It would be perfect. In any case they were going home for a week's break and if she planned it in advance, all of them could throw a grand farewell party. The more she thought about it, the more she liked the idea. In fact, she wanted to tell everyone right away but couldn't because Leila should not even get a hint of what was cooking in Tiana's mind.

The moment Leila went to the bathroom, Tiana told everyone about her plan.

'Guys what do you think about throwing a farewell party for Leila during the vacations?' asked Tiana excitedly.

'Hey, that's a great idea. Sounds fun,' said Bella.

'Oh yessss! We can start planning right now so that we will be ready and set to bring it on during the break,' said Savera.

'C'mon guys, let's do it,' said Celia, nodding her head in agreement.

'Fine. I'll come up with some ideas and then I'll let you know about it,' said Tiana.

'O-kay! Even we will think up something,' said Aliya.

'Great! I hope it turns out well,' said Tiana.

'Don't worry, it will,' said Bella confidently.

'But she should not find out anything about this guys. We need to be very careful,' reminded Lilly.

Just then, Leila returned. The girls, very slyly changed the topic to the latest movie so that Leila could be fooled . . . it was acting at its best!

After a few seconds, Savera turned to Leila and said in a matter-of-fact way, 'Leila, I was just thinking. Now you don't even have to appear for Boards.'

'Oh yeah! I didn't even think about that!' said Leila, delighted at the thought.

༄

'I hate Rubin,' cried out Bella.

'Who the hell is Rubin?' asked Tiana who was bored already.

'Tia, how can you ask me that? Rubin is my new boyfriend!'

said Bella, outraged that Tiana didn't know such an important piece of information.

'Oh yes, sorry. But you have had so many of them that I just can't remember their names now,' said Tiana honestly.

'That is very insulting,' said Bella, pouting.

'It is supposed to be a compliment. And how can you date a guy named Rubin? What kind of a name is Rubin?' asked Tiana.

'His name is not the point I am trying to make here,' said Bella, getting more furious by each passing second.

'All of you can't do this to me!' cried out Tiana.

'What are we doing to you?' asked Celia.

'You all can't fight with your boyfriends at the same time okay! It drives me nuts because you go on and on about it and I just can't console you all at the same time!' There! She finally vent it out.

'Please, this is no time for jokes T,' said Bella.

For the past half-an-hour, Tiana and Leila had been listening to their friends whine about the fights they had had with their boyfriends. Aliya and Zain had fought because Zain thought that Aliya was ignoring him a lot these days. Celia and Rehan had fought because Rehan had called Celia after classes but she hadn't gone to meet him because she had to study for a test and he felt offended. Tiana was yet to find out Bella's problem.

'So what did Rubin do?' asked Tiana dully.

'He said that I talk to him very rudely,' said Bella angrily.

'That's it? He thinks that you talk to him rudely and you fought over it?' asked Tiana in disbelief.

'That is the stupidest reason to fight over,' said Leila.

'No, it just started from this. Then I told him that he is very rude to me too and it got louder and louder until we were like screaming at each other,' said Bella weakly.

Tiana stifled a yawn. She didn't have the time for all this. She was really sleepy. For the past one week, she had literally become an owl. She had been staying awake till late to plan the farewell party. She couldn't do all this during the day because she had to study for various tests or finish her prep. If not that, then Leila was always around and Tiana wanted this party to be a complete surprise for Leila. That's why she had to be extra careful.

The good news was that Tiana had worked out the details for the party and was ready to put her plans into action as soon as their holiday break started. It was just three days away. The excitement of getting out of school was reaching its peaks. The only downer was that when all of them would return to school, Leila would not be coming with them. Tiana was still not okay with this huge change in her life. After all, her best friend was going away. Not that she wasn't being supportive . . . it was going to be a great new adventure for Leila. Tiana was happy for her. That's why she wanted to say goodbye to her friend as happily as possible through the surprise farewell party.

'Let's do something fun tonight guys! It is my last Saturday night in school,' said Leila.

'Like what?' asked Tiana.

Leila got up from Tiana's bed and went and turned on the music.

'Like dance!' said Leila happily.

All of them rushed to the empty area around the music system and started to dance. Other girls were staring at them with baffled looks. But within minutes, they found themselves shaking it to the music! All of them were dancing madly in the dorms. Tiana was enjoying herself to the core. While dancing, Tiana felt that one moment of slight pain when she realised that she would really miss these days and fun times with Leila. However, the thought was cut short as soon as one of Tia's favourite tracks started playing. After fifteen minutes of loud music and crazy dancing, they were forced to turn off the music at the shrill and threatening screams of their matron.

The next day, they got up late . . . all thanks to a glorious day called Sunday. They went down to the café and decided to spend most of the morning there. But soon, a junior guy came with a message for Bella.

'Bella, Rubin wants you to meet him near the art room,' said the boy.

'Tell him to go to hell,' said Bella tersely.

'He said just come and talk to him once,' said the boy nervously.

'Bella, it's okay. Go and sort it out,' said Lilly.

'Oh, alright,' said Bella, getting up reluctantly.

After Bella left, another boy came with a message for Aliya.

'Aliya, Zain is calling you. He is near the science lab,' said the boy, and without waiting for a reply he walked off.

That is how boyfriends call their girlfriends when they want to talk. Sending young boys as messengers because they are too cool and important to come and call themselves. When they wanted an argument, they sent some junior boy with a message. When they want to make up they send a junior boy as a messenger. These guys were too shy or did not have the guts to come out and actually face the girls. At least that's what Tiana liked to think.

'I am not going,' said Aliya.

'Come on Aliya, even Bella has gone to sort out everything,' said Leila.

So even Aliya left. Soon, just Leila, Lilly and Tiana were left.

'Sorry, your last Sunday in school will be with just us,' said Lilly.

'Its cool. But seriously, I will really miss this place and all of you,' said Leila.

'All the dumb stuff we do?' asked Tiana.

'That's for sure. Like climbing down a khud!' replied Leila.

'That was a classic example!' grinned Lilly.

'Won't you miss giving us dares?' asked Tiana.

'Yes, I will miss that the most,' replied Leila cheerfully.

'We will miss that the least for sure,' said Lilly.

'The very least!' added Tiana, 'But you did give the best dares. Give me some whacky ideas before you go okay?'

'No way! Think of them yourself,' laughed Leila.

Now that only three of them were left it was not so much fun hanging out at the café. So they went back to the dorms. Around lunch time 'the daters' came back to dorms. They were much more cheerful.

'Looks like you solved your problems,' said Tiana.

'I did. Do you want to know how?' asked Bella.

'No no no please!' said Tiana quickly. She was almost begging to be spared of the torture!

'How rude!' said Bella.

'I am sorry, but once you start you just don't stop,' said Tiana.

'Guys we are going home tomorrow,' said Leila, changing the subject.

'Finally we are getting out of school for some time. I am getting so sick of tests and lectures,' said Aliya.

'These will be my last holidays with you all, so we should make the most of this break. Promise?' asked Leila.

'Promise,' replied Bella.

∽

'Guys, come on! We just have two more hours,' said Tiana.

They had been preparing for Leila's farewell party. It had been a day since they had reached home. They were having the party in Bella's garden. The weather was good and that's why they decided to have it outdoors. Bella was going to go and pick up Leila, telling her that they were going to see a movie. And then Bella would pretend that she had forgotten her cell phone at home and that's how she would get Leila to her house.

Tiana and Savera had planned everything according to what Leila liked. The food was naturally Italian and the decorations were in red . . . even balloons and other stuff. (That was Leila's favourite colour.) All of them were dressed in red too. Everyone who liked Leila had come and many people liked Leila. Tiana just wished that everything would work out alright.

It did work. Around six, Bella returned with Leila and Leila was completely caught off guard! She was really surprised but she loved it. Everything was prefect. Their parents had come over as well. They played Truth and Dare again for the last time with Leila and danced all evening. Sid and Leila were together at last and both of them were enjoying themselves. Sid had been shocked at first when he found out about Leila shifting to Paris. But he had hidden his disappointment pretty well and had helped them with the party.

By the end of it when Leila was thanking everyone, she started to cry. Seeing her, Bella started crying too and soon all of them joined in. The boys started making fun of them so they asked them to get lost.

'Thanks for doing this Tiana,' said Leila.

'Hey, that's what friends are for,' smiled Tiana.

'I know. I will miss you so much!' said Leila.

∽

If Tiana had surprised Leila, then what Leila and the rest of her friends did stunned her even more. The thing was that Tiana's fifteenth birthday was just two days after the farewell party. Tiana was not in the mood for another party. So she was just planning to take her friends out for a movie and lunch but all this while, when Tiana had been planning the farewell, Leila had been planning her birthday party!

When she reached Savera's house, she was flabbergasted to find a party waiting for her. The moment she reached, everyone screamed 'Happy birthday Tiana!'

'Oh my God! I don't believe this!' said Tiana, looking around the garden.

'Surprised?' asked Leila.

'More than ever! Leila, for how long have you been planning this?' asked Tiana.

'Since I found out about Paris. I wanted to give you a last surprise . . . and dare.'

'That's when I started planning your farewell party too.'

'So both of you are surprised now, aren't you?' asked Bella.

'How come you managed to plan both the parties at the same time and still managed to keep it a secret?' asked Tiana, amazed because her friends were not very good with keeping a secret a secret.

'We can be very surprising at times,' said Savera.

'Well, you've actually proved it today,' smiled Tiana.

'Thanks!' said Lilly.

'Just one question . . . why are all the boys dressed in black and you girls in pink?' asked Tiana curiously.

'Because pink and black or one of them is your favourite colour,' said Leila.

'It is?' asked Tiana, startled.

'Yes, don't you know what's your favourite colour?' asked Bella.

'No I don't actually. That's why I'm "finding it". Remember?' said Tiana, 'And why do you think that I like pink or black?'

'Because you always buy black or pink clothes,' said Leila.

'And shoes,' added Bella.

'Your room is done up in pink and black,' said Aliya.

'You even have pink or black hats, gloves, belts and watches. Nobody needs so much pink or black around them until they like these colours,' pointed out Savera.

'Even if that doesn't satisfy you, then I just think that pink and black suit you and you should choose one of them as your favourite colour. So which one will it be?' asked Leila, 'Pink or black?'

Tough. Clearly, her friends had given this a lot of thought. At least they had made things easier by short listing two colours. Now she had to decide which one. Hmm ... She went to get a soda while thinking about this when someone interrupted her thoughts.

'Happy birthday Tia!'

'Thanks Karam!'

'Tia, I am sorry for the way I have been acting around you,' said Karam guiltily.

'Its okay, I guess.'

'It's just that now I feel I shouldn't have told you about any of this,' said Karam, a little uncomfortably.

'Karam, how come Sid knew about this?' asked Tiana.

'He told you?' asked Karam, taken aback by this question.

'Oh don't worry! He told me after you had already asked me out,' said Tiana.

'Oh!' said Karam softly, 'He has known about it for quite some time.'

'How long?' asked Tiana.

'About a year or something I guess,' said Karam.

'A year? You have liked me for a year and it is only now that you asked me out?' asked Tiana, gaping like a goldfish.

'Hey, it was really tough for me to tell you about it. You always treated me like a friend. So it was ... ,' trailed off Karam.

'Yeah, I guess it must have been a little tough for you,' said Tiana.

'Anyway, it doesn't matter now. You don't feel the same way about me. I get it.'

Now was her only chance to tell him about how she really felt. Should she tell him? But before she could make up her mind she chickened out.

'I will see you around I guess,' said Karam.

'Oh yeah, great,' said Tiana, and walked back to where her friends were sitting.

Long after the party got over, Tiana and Leila were sitting and gossiping in Tiana's room. Leila was staying over for the night.

'Tiana, now that I am going away, I just want to say something to you,' said Leila, very seriously.

'Sure. What is it?'

'Now I don't know for how long your "finding it" theory will continue because no matter what you do, you will keep changing as you grow older. But I just want you to know that you know yourself better than most of us know ourselves.'

'Come on Leila,' began Tiana but she was interrupted.

'It is true T. Think about it yourself. You are so sure about what you want. You refuse to do something if you don't want to. Tell me, how do you refuse to drink? Refused to even try it,' said Leila.

'Because I don't want to,' said Tiana plainly.

'Even if everyone around you is drinking? Even if they mock you at times for not trying it?' asked Leila again.

'Yes, even then. I think its stupid to ruin our bodies at such a young age.'

'See what I mean? You don't even give in to peer pressure! You don't date even though so many are dying to date you. Why?' questioned Leila.

'I don't want to date just for the heck of it. I have to actually like someone genuinely before dating them,' said Tiana, a little defensively.

'It didn't matter even though the guys started saying that you are not dating because you are not attracted to boys, right?' asked Leila.

'No it didn't matter because it wasn't true!' said Tiana.

'You didn't even feel insulted?' asked Leila.

'At first I felt a little insulted and frustrated at the wrong accusations but then it didn't matter. They are just a bunch of losers.'

'See, it didn't matter to you because you are so sure of yourself and you are confident about who you are and what you think. If they had thought about any of us like that we would have cried for weeks or been embarrassed about it at least. We would have reacted like that because we are not like you. We are not strong enough to say no. But you are Tia. That's all I am trying to tell you. You already know your true self and feelings. It was only for some time that you were not in touch with them and that made you feel a little lost. Don't try so hard to find yourself because you were never lost,' finished Leila.

Wow! How come she hadn't thought of all this before? She didn't want to boast or anything but a lot of what Leila just said was true.

'Tia, what are you thinking about?' asked Leila.

'About what you just said.'

'That's good! Think about it. I am going to the washroom.'

Tiana did think about it. So she tried to do what Leila had asked her to do . . . to not try so hard. She sat on her bed and thought about which one would it be. Pink or black? After five minutes, she knew which one was her favourite. It was not a colour but it was colours. She loved both the colours equally. Why did she have to have only one favourite colour? We could like as many things as we wanted to. Leila was right. We keep changing and nothing was permanent. So, as long as she liked pink and black, it was all good. Who knows? Maybe her next favourite colour would be orange! Everyone needed a change after some time. The trick is to always be truthful to yourself and that does wonders to your confidence.

'Leila, I know which one is my favourite colour,' cried out Tiana.

'Which one?'

'It's not pink or black. Its pink and black,' said Tiana.

'Cool. Both of them huh? They make a very sexy combo. So how many questions are left on your list now? Try to complete it before I leave.'

'Maybe I will,' replied Tiana. It was true. Most of the basic questions on her list were answered. She was feeling extremely happy. She had had the most amazing birthday with her friends and finally, after months of soul searching, she felt that she understood herself. It was a great feeling. Great enough to make you sleepy. By the time Leila got out of the washroom, Tiana was fast asleep.

SIX

'Tiana, I am leaving. But I want all of you to reach on time, okay?' cried out Sid from outside Tiana's bedroom door.

'Fine! We'll be on time. Don't worry,' said Tiana for like the tenth time.

It was finally Sid's big night. It was two days after Tiana's birthday. Sid was hyper energetic and excited. He wanted everything to be perfect. Well, it was important for him and that's why everyone was listening to him for once.

'What's wrong with Sid? He needs to calm down,' said Savera.

'Try telling him that!' said Bella.

'No way! He might just chop me into little pieces!' said Savera.

All of them were ready. Tiana was wearing a pink and black knee length dress. She was in a very good mood and wanted to celebrate. It was for no particular reason . . . just a general feeling of euphoria. She was feeling very happy because these holidays were the best ever for her. She was enjoying each day with her friends. The only sad bit was that Leila was going away. Other than that, life was great without tests and house mistresses and teachers. Just then Leila came into the room. (She had been with Sid till now.)

'I just came to tell you that you have to leave in five minutes okay? Hurry,' said Leila.

'You are talking like Sid,' said Lilly.

'Can't help it. I have been with Sid for the entire day,' smiled Leila.

'Don't worry, we are ready. Tell your boyfriend too,' said Tiana.

'I am leaving with Sid right now,' said Leila, and then she hurried out of the room.

'What's gotten into them?' asked Bella.

'They know us very well. That's why they know we will take ages to get ready and we will be late,' said Savera.

'So let's go and prove them wrong,' said Tiana.

They rushed downstairs. Tiana's mom and dad were driving them to the party. Leila and Sid had already left with Karam.

'Girls, you are looking great,' said Tiana's mom.

'Thanks mom. Let's go or Sid will just kill us,' said Tiana.

'Good idea!' smiled her dad.

They reached the party on time and Sid rushed towards them the moment he saw them enter.

'Thank God you are on time,' said Sid, relieved.

'Sid relax! Breathe, will you?' said Tiana.

'Listen to your sister,' said Bella.

'Yeah whatever! Your table is right in the front,' said Sid.

'Chill out. You go and do what you have to do and stop worrying about us,' said Tiana's mom.

'O-kay. I will see you around.'

They went and sat down at their table when Aryan, Rehan, Zain, Rubin and much to Tiana's disappointment, Veer joined them.

'What on earth is Veer doing here?' Tiana whispered to Leila.

'Come on Tiana, we just can't leave him out because Bella dumped him!' Leila whispered back.

'Why not? That's a very good reason to leave him out. You know he is a jerk.' Tiana couldn't tolerate the sight of this creep. She could do anything to keep him out of her way.

'Just ignore him,' said Bella, who had apparently overheard the conversation.

'Tia I just wanted to apologise,' said Veer, just when Tiana wanted to ignore him more than anything.

'Don't start your crap and I swear it . . . if you call me Tia one more time, you will regret it,' snapped Tiana.

'Hey Tiana, he is saying sorry in front of everyone. Come on stop your fight now,' said Aryan in a tone which said: 'He's a boy. How dare a girl treat him like dirt? It's like a matter of broken pride for all the guys if even one of them is losing in a fight with a girl.'

'Excuse me! So what if he is saying sorry in front of everyone. He spread cheap rumours about me amongst everyone too. Am I the only one who remembers that?' said Tiana angrily.

'Please don't spoil everyone's mood Veer. And you too Aryan,' said Bella.

Both of them decided to stay quiet. Shortly after that, Sid's album was released. They didn't see much of him during the party because he was busy with the press conference and his duties.

'Leila,' said Tiana.

'What?'

'You are drinking again,' said Tiana, pointing at her glass.

'Hey, it is just champagne. I am celebrating!' said Leila.

'You will never understand!' said Tiana with a dismissive shake of her head.

'I guess I won't,' said Leila. 'Besides, I am going to Paris. Over there people drink wine with every meal!'

She gave up again. This topic had been discussed so many times and each time Tiana had lost. Now she had completely given up the hope of making her friends give up drinking. She got up to go to the washroom when she saw Karam. Something just made her walk up to him to tell him the truth.

'Hi Tiana!' said Karam, when he saw her coming towards him.

'Karam, before I chicken out, I have to tell you something,' said Tiana quickly.

'Umm okay . . . go ahead.'

'The day you asked me out, I was shocked. Completely shocked out of my wits because I always thought of you as Leila's elder brother and a friend.'

'I know and it's okay. You don't have to say sorry Tia. Please.'

'No, I have not come to say sorry. What I mean is that till then I didn't even think that this was possible,' said Tiana.

'What wasn't possible?' asked Karam. His eyes were beginning to sparkle with interest.

'See now you will just think of me as a stupid . . . '

'No I will not think that you are stupid,' interrupted Karam quickly.

'But you don't even know what I am going to say,' said Tiana, a little taken aback.

'What didn't you think was possible Tia?' asked Karam again.

'That we both could ever go out.' Tiana was feeling really awkward now.

'Now what do you think?' asked Karam, slowly looking directly at Tiana.

This was tougher than she had thought.

'Karam, it is really weird for me to say this but I think I . . . oh, forget it! I am sorry, just forget it . . . .' She turned around to leave when Karam spoke.

'Tiana, you can't do this. You have to finish what you have started. I will go mad trying to guess what you were trying to say. Just say it. Can't be that hard . . . ' He couldn't finish because Tiana interrupted him.

'I like you too,' said Tiana softly.

'What?' Karam looked stunned.

'You heard me. I just wanted you to know that before you left, that's all.'

'Why didn't you tell me when I asked you out?' asked Karam, finally smiling.

'At that time I was just shocked like I told you. Before that, it hadn't ever crossed my mind that I could like you more than a friend,' said Tiana, turning to go.

'Hey wait! You can't go,' said Karam.

'Why not? I told you what I had to. It is done now,' said Tiana.

'It is still not done. Tia, will you go out with me now?' asked Karam.

This was something she was definitely not expecting.

'We can't date each other. Karam, you are going to Paris!' said Tiana not able to believe that this conversation was actually happening.

'What if I told you that I am not going?' smiled Karam.

'Then I will ask you to stop lying,' said Tiana.

'I am not lying Tiana. I still don't believe it that all of you actually believe that we are moving to Paris,' laughed Karam.

'What's there to believe! You are going right?' asked Tiana, confused by what Karam had just said.

'Are you kidding me? Leila has been lying to all of you about this entire Paris thing.'

'What? She what?' asked Tiana, stunned.

'That's right. The day our parents came to school, my little sister lied to all of you about this whole Paris thing. You all actually believed her and that's why she asked our parents and me to play along,' grinned Karam.

'Are you telling me that you all are not moving to Paris?' asked Tiana, appalled.

'Yes, that's exactly what I am telling you.'

'This doesn't make any sense!' cried out Tiana.

'It doesn't?'

'Why did your parents come up to school then?' asked Tiana.

'Our parents just came with their friends for a break from work and they decided to stop by at the school and meet us. That's it. Not to withdraw us from school.'

'But your mom had started packing and everything,' said Tiana in disbelief.

'You haven't seen our house till now. Nothing is getting packed. We are not going to Paris Tia,' said Karam.

'Why has Leila been lying?' asked Tiana, still in shock.

'It is still April. She is making a fool out of all of you,' grinned Karam.

'I am going to kill your sister,' said Tiana curling her fist in mock anger. Inside, her heart was doing a spring dance!

'Be my guest!' said Karam with a glint of mischief in his eyes.

'And I am going to do it right now!' said Tiana.

'Wait. First you have to tell me. Now that you do like me and I am not moving to Paris, will you go out with me?' asked Karam in a serious tone.

She looked at him for a moment and then answered his question.

'Yes.'

She had never seen Karam smile like that before. She had never felt this happy before either. She was hoping that she didn't look moony eyed!

Five minutes later she went back to the table with Karam.

'Guys, I have to tell you all two very important things,' announced Tiana.

'Shoot,' said Bella.

'Firstly, I am going to kill my dearest friend Leila, because this woman is the biggest liar on earth!'

'Why is that?' asked Savera.

'Because she is NOT moving to Paris!' cried out Tiana.

Everyone was quiet for a few seconds. For a moment, it looked like all their eyes would pop out . . . just like the way it happens in cartoons! Then they all started firing questions at Leila.

'I don't believe this!' said Lilly.

'Leila, is this true?' asked Bella, rolling her eyes at Leila.

'You have been lying about this?' wailed Savera.

Everyone was staring at Leila and waiting for a reasonable explanation.

'Oh oh! So you all had to find it out someday,' laughed Leila.

'I don't believe you! We even threw you a farewell party!' said Tiana.

'I know and didn't we all have fun?' said Leila.

'You are so mean! You made us all feel so bad and now it turns out that it was for nothing at all,' said Aliya.

'Please don't get so angry guys. I am sorry. I just thought it will turn out to be a good laugh.' This topic continued for another ten minutes and then finally the attention turned to Tiana again.

'So Tiana, what was the second thing that you had to tell us? Please tell us now and take the heat off me. I can't bear it anymore!' Leila was literally begging.

'The second thing is that Karam and I are officially going around now,' said Tiana, smiling at her friends and enjoying the expressions of utter shock and bafflement on their faces.

After a lot of hoots from the guys and girls, Savera spoke up.

'Seriously, you are?' asked Savera.

'Yes we are,' replied Karam.

'Congratulation guys! Especially you Tiana! You're finally dating!' said Lilly.

'For how long has this been going on?' asked Aliya.

'I asked Tiana out before the Kick Off. She finally said yes fifteen minutes ago,' smiled Karam who was also blushing slightly.

'Tia, it took you so long to say yes?' asked Bella.

'I know. I am a little slow, ain't I?' smiled Tiana.

'All these years you were my "ultimate challenge" because I couldn't find the right guy for you. If only I had known that the right guy was my own brother!' said Leila, getting up from her chair. She went and hugged Tiana.

'Congrats Tia!' smiled Leila.

'Thank you but this does not mean that we will forgive you for this entire Paris thing.'

'What Paris thing?'

It was Sid.

'Sid, Leila is not going to Paris!' said Tiana.

'Really? Thank God! Wait a minute, you were punking us all this while?' asked Sid.

'Yes I was actually,' said Leila.

'How could we fall for it?' said Sid, 'But that's okay. I'm just relieved and happy that you are going to stay.'

He went and hugged Leila.

'By the way Sid, your sister is going out with my brother,' smiled Leila.

'You are?' asked Sid, stunned.

'I am.'

'Finally! Congrats!'

'To you too Sid, for your album,' said Tiana.

'Thanks! Okay, I know you all have been getting bored so I will be free within half-an-hour. Then we can go somewhere else' said Sid.

'Cool, that will be fun,' said Bella.

'Now I need to go and socialise. See you later!' said Sid, and he left the table.

'Leila, I am so happy that you are not going,' said Tiana. No matter how big a lie it was, it was truly relieving to know that Leila was not going to go.

'I was never going.'

'Oh oh-kay, don't rub it in.'

'Right. Sorry!'

'How come you managed to create this story and stick by it too?' asked Tiana.

'I don't know. I just came up with the story and you fell for it. And I continued it . . .'

Tiana definitely fell for it. But she was really happy to know that Leila would be staying. She had been very upset about this entire thing. It was for the first time that someone so close to her was going away. She didn't know when she would get to see her best friend again. But now, everything was fine. If any thing, Leila's joke has just made Tiana realise the importance of friends even more.

After forty-five minutes, Sid came back. Most of the people and the press had left.

'Let's go, I am free.'

'Where should we go?' asked Celia.

'How about Electric?' said Bella.

'Oh yes, let's go there,' Leila nodded in agreement.

'Electric it is,' said Aryan.

∽

They had been sitting in Electric for over an hour already.

'Remember the last days of the winter holidays when you guys pissed off Tiana?' asked Savera.

'That night we saw a never before seen version of Tiana,' said Bella.

'I can't believe it Aryan. You actually thought that Tiana was not attracted to boys!' exclaimed Savera.

'Now you can't think that because Tia has a boyfriend,' said Bella.

'Hey, we have already apologised to Tia,' said Rehan.

'And except for Veer, she has forgiven all of us,' said Aryan.

'Hold it! Enough about me. It's making me very uncomfortable,' said Tiana.

'But you are the most interesting person amongst us,' said Celia.

'So T, how is your "finding it" mission going on?' asked Sid.

'It's great. I am really happy about it,' said Tiana, smiling from ear to ear.

'That's good.'

'Hey it is already 11 pm,' said Savera checking her watch.

'So what?' asked Aryan.

'I need to go home. My mom wants me back by 11.30.'

'You are going already?' asked Bella.

'I have to. Who can drop me off?' asked Savera.

'Even I need to go home,' said Aliya.

'Come on, stay for a while. Please!' pleaded Leila.

'No I have to go,' said Aliya.

'I can drop you off,' said Sid.

'Now why are you going?' asked Leila.

'I am just tired Leila. I want to go home and take a bath,' said Sid.

'Does anyone else want to leave?' asked Karam.

'I think I want to go too,' said Zain.

'Me too,' said Rubin.

'Me three,' said Veer.

'Come on guys. Why are you all leaving? Stay,' cried out Bella.

'Tough luck Bella,' said Tiana.

'Yeah, they will not stay. Chill! We can hang out here,' said Lilly.

'Yeah,' said Leila.

'Tiana, are you staying?' asked Karam.

'Yes, I am. But all of you can go,' said Tiana.

'Are you sure?'

'Yes of course.'

'Fine. Call me when you want to come back home. I'll come and pick you up,' said Sid.

'Thanks a lot! I will.'

So Sid, Karam, Rubin, Zain, Veer, Savera and Aliya left.

'It is just us now,' said Bella.

'Hey Tia, what's the next question on your list. Maybe we can help you again,' said Celia.

'No, you can't . . . not this time.'

'Why not? Try us,' said Leila.

'Before helping me, tell me which is your favourite quote,' said Tiana.

They were quiet for a few seconds. In the middle of the night, this question was the last thing they could answer. After a few moments of acting like they were thinking, they finally quit.

'You are right. We can't help you with this one,' agreed Celia.

'Sid and Karam are good with this,' said Bella.

The question was soon forgotten and then they just talked away into the night . . . morning rather. They talked about everything under the sun. So much so that Tiana didn't even remember what they had been talking about. Exams, teachers, fights, crushes, weird experiences . . . you name it, they talked about it. After all, when you are with friends, everything feels just great.

Finally around 2 am they got out of Electric. Everyone except Tiana was drunk. They were singing and walking towards the parking lot. As soon as they reached the car, the gang stuffed themselves inside the car. Tiana didn't get inside.

'What are you waiting for Tia? Come on, let's go-o-o,' yawned Bella.

'You know what? I don't think that would be such a good idea,' hesitated Tiana.

'What? You want to party some more?" asked Rehan, squinting at her.

'No, that's not what I meant Rehan. What I did mean is that all of you are drunk.'

'Come on Tia, we are not that drunk,' said Aryan sleepily.

'Still . . . '

For a moment, she felt stupid for standing outside and refusing to get into the car. They were not that drunk . . . but they were a little tipsy. She didn't have to make such a big deal out of it.

'Fine, I will come,' said Tiana, still hesitating.

'Thank you, we're honoured!' said Bella.

Tiana was about to sit inside when the same voice inside her head (which had stopped her from drinking) stopped her from getting inside the car. She had started her 'finding it' theory just so that she could do what she really felt like doing in these kind of situations and she didn't want to sit in that car.

'NO.'

'No?'

'Sorry, but I can't sit in that car. I just can't. Something is scaring me. I have already called Sid. Maybe he should drive us home,' said Tiana nervously.

'Oh God! You are talking like my mom now. Just get in the car silly,' said Rehan. He was already looking groggy eyed.

'As far as I am concerned, I just don't think it's safe! If you want to carry on, then go. I won't stop you but I will not get into that car. Sid is coming to pick me up anyway,' said Tiana icily.

'Rehan, don't talk to Tia like that,' said Celia.

'Tia, it's okay. The thing is that we can't leave you alone so late at night,' said Leila.

Just then Tiana's cell phone beeped. She read the message.

'It is Sid's message. He will be here in five minutes. Don't worry about me. I will go and wait inside. You guys carry on,' said Tiana.

'Are you sure?' asked Bella.

'Absolutely.'

'Fine. Then we will give you a call tomorrow,' said Celia.

'Bye! Please drive safely,' said Tiana. She was feeling very uneasy for some reason. Something told her that this just wasn't right.

'Not again! I think you don't trust my driving skills,' said Rehan.

'I don't trust any one's driving skills when they are drunk,' said Tiana calmly.

'Fine then!'
'Bye Tiana!' said Leila.
'Bye!'
Rehan drove the car out of the parking lot and got onto the main road. As he drove away, Tiana wondered whether her worried to death mind was over working or whether the car seemed to zig-zag its way down the road. Tiana was just about to turn and go inside when . . .

That's when it happened.
Just when she was about to put her foot on the steps, she heard the squeal of the tyres as the car suddenly picked up speed. She turned around to see what was happening. She could see the car reaching a blind turn. She could feel her heart beats racing to a dangerous speed. Rehan didn't honk when he was supposed to. He didn't even slow down. Before she could even think of anything, an SUV came from around the corner and both the cars collided with an ear-splitting BANG.

The bang startled her out of her senses. It didn't register at first but when it did, Tiana felt faint with panic. Tiana was not sure if the shrill scream she had just heard had escaped from her mouth or if it was by someone from the car. Terrified, she ran towards the car. She was desparately praying and hoping that her friends were safe. Her legs felt like jelly and she broke into a cold sweat. The whole scene felt like a scene taken right out of a nightmare.

When Tiana reached the spot, the scene she saw was so horrifying that it has refused to leave Tiana's memory ever since. The bonnet was completely smashed and the windshield had shattered into a zillion pieces of glass. She ran around the car frantically and tried to open its doors. To her utter disappointment and fright, they were jammed. She tried to peep inside the car and see if anyone was conscious. Her mind went blank. Damn it! What was she going to do? Ambulance. She would have to call the hospital. She took out her cell phone from her bag. Her hands were shivering uncontrollably.

Just then, Sid reached the spot.

What the hell happened?' Sid look stunned. He gaped at the mangled car and couldn't believe what he was seeing.

'Thank God you have come! Call some hospital. We need an ambulance right now! Hurry! Call some one! We are wasting time!' cried out Tiana hysterically.

'I'll call for an ambulance,' said Sid.

'Hurry up! Hurry hurry hurry!' said the trembling Tiana.

'Tiana, help me open these doors,' said a familiar voice.

Tiana turned around and saw Karam.

'Karam! These doors are jammed,' sobbed Tiana.

'Relax! Just try and pull okay?' said Karam calmly.

How could he be so calm? His sister was inside! Leila could be hurt badly. Any one of them could be dead. The moment this thought came to Tiana's mind she started to cry uncontrollably but she continued to pull hard at the door. Finally, one of them opened.

All of the people in the car were unconscious. And there was blood . . . so much blood and glass. Bella, who was closest to the door, had her head in her lap. Tiana pulled her up carefully. Bella had a sharp glass piece stuck in her cheek and it was bleeding heavily. Tiana was about to pull it out when Karam stopped her.

'Don't! Let the doctors do this,' said Karam, pulling her away from the car.

'Yes you are right,' sniffed Tiana.

'Just to be on the safe side, we should not touch any of them. We might end up doing more harm than help,' cautioned Karam.

'Okay. But they are all wounded . . . badly wounded,' said Tiana.

'Yes, they are. Who was driving?'

'Rehan.'

'I hope he'll be alright,' said Karam.

'Can't we do anything to help them right now?' asked Tiana. She had never felt so helpless before. Her first instinct was to just pull them all out of the car. Even if she wanted to, sense said that she shouldn't.

'Not till the paramedics get here,' said Karam.

'It's nightmarish! I can't believe I've just witnessed this. The way they banged into that car . . . ,' Tiana couldn't finish.

'Stop it. Don't recall it Tia. Just don't. It won't help you and right now you need to be strong,' said Karam. His calmness during this moment of crisis was indeed very necessary.

Tiana just nodded. After five minutes, which seemed like centuries, two ambulances arrived. Never before had she found the sound of an ambulance so comforting.

One by one they pulled out everyone from the car very carefully. Celia's leg was stuck. She was sitting in the front seat. It took them ten minutes to pull out Rehan from the driving seat.

Tiana couldn't bear the sight of her wounded friends being taken out like this. They seemed lifeless. Each second felt like she was in some sort of a torture chamber. She prayed fervently. Her only prayer was that all of them should be okay. Never in her life had she felt so desperately helpless.

'Tiana, dad is coming,' said Sid.

Tiana and Karam could not really help much. Tiana went to check up on her friends who were now lying unconscious on the stretchers. There was blood everywhere. Tiana felt weak and sick in the tummy. Everything seemed like a haze. It was hellish. Almost everyone's face and arms had cuts and bruises. The worst were of Rehan and Celia. Shards of glass from the windshield had cut them in many places.

Tiana didn't know about any internal injuries but hoped that her friends would have been spared of those. Nothing could be worse than seeing your closest friends lying unconscious on stretchers, looking like they would never open their eyes again. Five minutes ago, they had been happily singing and kidding around. And now, they were covered in their own blood!

Again and again the thought that she could have been in this car and that she could be lying in a stretcher right now kept invading her mind.

She watched her friends being taken away in the ambulance. She felt numb.

Within five minutes, Tiana's mom and dad showed up.

'Tia, are you alright?' asked her mother, equally worried and shaken.

'Mom!' Tiana hugged her mother. 'I am fine. I wasn't even in the car,' said Tiana.

'Let's go to the hospital,' said Sid.

'Yes. We need to go to the hospital mom,' said Tiana.

'Fine. Let's go.'

All her friends were admitted in the emergency room. The doctors were desperately running around from one room to another. They didn't have the time or opportunity to give Tiana and her family a word of hope. Tiana caught just a glimpse of Leila and Celia when the doctor had opened the door to go inside the room. They were still unconscious and had a lot of tubes sticking out of their arms and noses. They had been sitting outside for over an hour after which her mom came up to her.

'Tiana, there is no point in hanging around here now. Let's go home honey. We can come back tomorrow.' Tiana could just see her mom mouthing something but couldn't hear anything. She just nodded as if by habit. She didn't get up. She was too engrossed in her thoughts. Her mind was screening the worst scenarios. Everything around her seemed to be swirling. It was toe-curling, spine-chilling frightening. Optimism was just not willing to enter her mind. Why were they still unconscious?

'Let's go Tia,' urged her mother.

Suddenly, Tiana snapped out of her rigmarole of flashbacks, frightening thoughts and scary scenes. She slowly got up to leave.

On the way back home, there was so much going through her mind. Would her friends be alright? What had saved her from being in that car? What? Then the scene of the accident played through her mind again . . . the squeal of the tires, the shriek of the brakes . . . the heart-stopping bang. To add to the misery, Mr Guilt was wreaking havoc in her mind. Why couldn't she have tried a little harder and persuaded them not to drive in that condition? Before she knew it, she was crying silently. To see those two cars crash into each other had been the worst thing to see. More so because the people you loved the most were inside one of them.

Tiana's mind seemed like a concoction of images from her past. Till now she had always wished that she would live her life to the utmost limit and experience everything. But an accident like this one was certainly not on the checklist of experiences in her mind. She desperately hoped and wished that never should she see something as horrible as this again. No one should ever have to see such a ghastly thing happen to the ones they care for. Yes, that was her greatest wish. Now she would have to go through a painful period of waiting, hoping and wishing to see what will happen to the people she cared for.

The moment she reached home, she went and locked herself in her bedroom and didn't come out for the next twelve hours.

SEVEN

'Please tell us what you saw?' asked one of the officers.

'Rehan was driving the car very fast but his driving was not steadly. When the car reached a blind turn, Rehan didn't honk and their car banged into an SUV coming from around the corner. That's what happened,' said Tiana plainly, trying hard to block out the images which accompanied this story.

'Was Rehan drunk?' asked the officer.

'Yes.'

'Why didn't anyone else drive then?'

'Everyone in that car was drunk,' said Tiana.

'Why weren't you in that car?'

'Because I chose not to. I felt it was not safe.'

'Why didn't you try and stop them?'

'I did. They just didn't listen,' said Tiana. Deep down, she could feel a thousand arrows of guilt pricking at her heart. She knew that she hadn't tried hard enough. If only she had tried, maybe things would have been different.

'That's about it,' said the officer, 'Thank you for your time.'

'No problem,' said Tiana, glad to be done with it.

After they left, her mother came in again.

'How did it go?'

'Fine. It was fine.' Tiana was feeling miserable inside but she managed to smile at her mom.

'Your friends are here to see you. Do you want to see them?' asked her mother.

'Sure, call them.'

After five minutes, Aliya, Savera, Karam, Rubin, Zain and Sid came into her room.

'Hi Tia! How are you feeling?' asked Savera.

'I am fine. The question is how are the ones in the hospital feeling?' asked Tiana.

'We wanted to talk to you but you have been in this room for the entire day,' said Aliya.

'I know. I was sleeping all this while.'

'Are you sure you're fine?' asked Karam softly, taking her hand into his.

'I wasn't. But now that you all are here, I feel much better,' said Tiana honestly. 'You guys are so lucky you didn't have to see it in front of your own eyes.'

'How did it happen?' asked Zain.

Tiana explained the whole incident to them as quickly as she could.

'It must have been very painful for them,' said Rubin.

'Did you go to the hospital?' asked Tiana.

'Yes. We did go,' replied Karam.

'What's happening? How are they doing now?' asked Tiana.

'Celia and Leila are still unconscious. The doctors said that when the cars banged into each other, their heads and necks got jerked pretty hard and that's what's causing some problems,' said Karam.

'So will they be alright?' asked Tiana.

'Yes, the doctors believe so,' said Sid.

'Thank God!' sighed Tiana, 'What about the rest of them?'

'Rehan has broken a few ribs and he has fractured his right arm and left leg.'

'Oh God!'

'Bella has fractured her right arm and has a very horrible cut on her cheek. Fortunately, Lilly and Aryan have escaped with minor cuts and bruises. Celia has fractured her right leg. Thankfully, nothing is very serious. The doctors say that it's a miracle that they've escaped the worst . . . lady luck had favoured them,' said Karam.

'I really want to go and meet them,' said Tiana.

'We all can go tomorrow morning,' said Aliya.

'For now, you just take rest,' said Sid.

'But I am fine!' protested Tiana.

'You scared us a lot when you didn't come out of your room for so long,' said Karam.

'I told you I was sleeping. Trust me, I am fine. I was just shaken up by what I had seen. I needed to sleep away the shock effect. That's all.'

'Tell me something?' asked Aliya.

'What?'

'How come you weren't in that car?' asked Aliya.

This was THE question on everyone's mind. But thanks to her 'finding it' quest she didn't have to think twice or make up something. Honesty worked for her.

'I felt it was too risky. I almost got into that car but I backed out just in time. I tried to stop them too but they weren't interested in what I had to say,' said Tiana.

'I know, how can they be?' scoffed Karam.

'Tia, we will come by your house in the morning and then we can go to the hospital,' said Savera.

'Great!' said Tiana.

'Bye and take care of yourself,' said Aliya.

'For the last time, I am fine,' said Tiana, a little irritated by now. She hated being fussed over.

'We know. Just take care of yourself,' said Karam.

'Okay I will.'

After her friends left, Tiana came out of her room. She was feeling a little weak but sitting in her room was not helping her either. Leila and Celia were still unconscious. That couldn't be good. At least the doctors thought that everything would be alright.

She went to the twins' room.

'Hi Tia, how are you feeling now?' asked Dhruv.

'I am fine. Thanks for the chocolate!'

'You are welcome,' said Daksh.

'What are you doing?' asked Tiana looking around.

Their floor was scattered with car tracks and dinky cars.

'Do you want to play with us?' asked Dhruv.

'No thanks. I can't play with cars,' smiled Tiana.

'So get your old Barbie dolls and then Superman and Spiderman can save your dolls,' said Dhruv excitedly .

'And then your Barbie can kiss Spiderman when he is hanging upside down from the wall,' said Daksh. Clearly, Hollywood's super-hero movies were running through his blood!

'What? Okaaay, both of you, stop watching so many movies!' exclaimed Tiana.

'Why? What's wrong with that?' asked Daksh.

'Have you both been stealing my Barbie doll so than Spiderman can kiss her?' asked Tiana suspiciously.

'No.'

'Stop lying!'

'Oh well, we did. But only once,' said Daksh.

'Only once, hmmmm . . . .?'

'Actually we have stolen . . . I mean borrowed your dolls many times,' confessed Dhruv.

Tiana smiled at her brothers. Shamelessly cute and adorably mischievous . . . her baby brothers were just too sweet to be scolded. She had been with them for five minutes and she was feeling much better already.

'Are you angry?' asked Daksh nervously.

'No I am not angry. I just thought that girls play with dolls,' said Tiana, heading for the door and chuckling to herself.

She got the reaction she had been itching for.

'Hey, we don't play with dolls,' said Daksh, sounding disgusted at the thought.

'Yes you do!' sang Tiana, closing the door behind her.

'No we don't!' they shot back.

She went back to her room. Her mom was waiting for her.

'Where did you go?' asked her mother.

'To the twins' room.'

'What are they up to now?'

'You won't believe it! They want my old dolls so that Spiderman can kiss them hanging upside down from the wall,' laughed Tiana.

'Oh God! The ideas these boys get! They are impossible!' said her mother, partially laughing and partially amazed.

'They are adorable,' said Tiana.

'I am glad that you are finally smiling honey,' said her mother.

'Now that I know that everyone is going to be alright, I am feeling fine.'

'Don't worry, they will be fine. Good night!'

'Good night mom!'

∽

'Oooh, that's a nasty cut Bella,' exclaimed Tiana.

'Tell me about it!' replied Bella in a robotic voice. She couldn't open her mouth because of the deep cut on her cheek.

'But it is not that bad,' said Aliya.

'Yes it is! My face and my life is ruined,' said Bella sadly.

'It will be fine. The mark will fade away slowly.' Tiana was trying her best to console her.

'Then at least my teenage years are spoilt.'

That is true. Clearly that mark would take a lot of time to fade. Tiana couldn't say this to Bella though.

'How are you doing Lilly?' asked Savera.

'I am perfectly alright. Me and Aryan just got a few bruises and scratches. We were lucky,' replied Lilly.

'It was so scary,' said Bella.

'What exactly happened to Rehan?' asked Savera.

'Rehan started driving at break-neck speed. We asked him to slow down but it was like he couldn't hear us and then WHAM! His break-neck speed has nearly literally broken some part of everyone now!' explained Aryan.

'Don't think about it,' said Tiana.

'Tia, you saw us, didn't you?' asked Aryan.

'I saw everything. That's why I don't want to think about it.'

'I guess you are right but we should have listened to you,' said Bella quietly.

There you go again. Mr Guilt comes galloping in again. Tiana had been dreading this. She didn't want to hear her friends say that they should have listened to her. After all, even she hadn't tried hard enough to stop them.

'Forget it. Where is Rehan?' asked Tiana, changing the subject.

'Come with me, I will take you to his room,' volunteered Karam.

Rehan's room was the last room down the corridor. He was reading a magazine. His right hand and left leg were in a cast.

'Hi Rehan!' said Tiana.

He looked up and saw all of them.

'Hi Tia!'

'How are you feeling now?' asked Aliya.

'I feel pain. Everywhere. It really hurts,' said Rehan weakly.

'It will get better,' said Tiana.

'Tiana, I just want to say sorry,' started Rehan but Tiana interrupted him.

'Don't feel sorry, please.'

'How can I not feel sorry? You warned us but we didn't listen to you. I am feeling so guilty. Because of my carelessness, everyone got hurt,' said Rehan. The corners of his mouth looked as if they were pulled down permanently. A sad and guilty look flashed across his face.

'Everyone makes mistakes Rehan. Even I didn't try very hard to stop you. I should have but I didn't and look what happened.' Tiana's guilty conscious mind just had to speak out.

'Come on, do you think we would have listened to you? And I am sorry for saying that you were talking like my mother,' said Rehan.

'It's okay. Forget it. Just tell me exactly what happened?' asked Tiana.

'I don't know. I kind of blacked out. By the time I realised what was happening it was too late to control it.'

'Do you think it was because you were drunk?' asked Karam.

'Yes, I am sure that was the reason because normally I don't doze off while driving.'

They were just sitting and talking when Sid came in.

'Guys, the doctors have allowed us to meet Leila and Celia.'

Leila and Celia had gained consciousness last night. But the doctors hadn't allowed visitors to see them.

'That's great, let's go.' After saying a quick goodbye to Rehan, Tiana rushed out of the room.

Leila and Celia were in the same room. They were lying on their beds with their eyes closed. But as soon as Tiana reached the bed, Leila opened her eyes.

'Leila! Thank God you are fine!' said Tiana. It was such a relief to see Leila finally open her eyes.

'Did you have any doubt about it?' smiled Leila.

'Hehe! Doubts? You wouldn't want to know what kind of a cauldron my mind had become in the past two days! But I know that nothing can happen to my friends,' smiled Tiana. Clearly, pessimism had been thrown out of the window now.

Just then, Leila's parents came in and the doctor asked the rest of them to leave the room. But Tiana was satisfied. Leila and Celia would be alright. Everyone was alright. Thank God!

They spent the rest of the day in finishing their packing. They had to return to school the next day. Lilly, Bella and Aryan had permission to return to school as well. But Leila, Celia and Rehan had to remain in the hospital for a few more days.

Tiana went to the hospital again in the evening. Leila was propped up against her pillows but Celia was sleeping.

'Hi Leila!'

'Hi, I wasn't expecting you,' smiled Leila.

'We are going back to school tomorrow. I just wanted to say bye. I hope I am not disturbing you,' asked Tiana.

'Disturbing me! From what? This hospital is the most boring place on this earth. I'm just thanking my stars that you've come!' said Leila.

'I am so happy that all of you are alright,' said Tiana.

'I am so sorry for not listening to you, Tiana,' said Leila softly.

'Now don't start that . . . not again, pleeeease!' sighed Tiana.

'What are you talking about?' asked Leila, looking confused.

'Everyone has been saying this to me. That they should have listened to me,' said Tiana.

'We should have,' said Leila.

'But you didn't! So think of the past only if its remembrance gives pleasure,' stated Tiana.

'You just quoted Shakespeare!' said Leila.

'I did?' asked Tiana, wondering how she could have ever remembered anything from Shakespeare.

'Yes, what you just said—think of the past only if blah, blah! Shakespeare wrote that,' said Leila.

'How do you know that?' asked Tiana.

'Where did you hear that?' asked Leila.

'I read it somewhere and I liked it and that's how I remember it,' said Tiana simply.

'Do you know what this means?' asked Leila.

'What does this mean?' asked Tiana, still not understanding what Leila was trying to say.

'It is an answer to one of your questions Tia!' said Leila brightly.

Then it hit her.

'My favourite quote! Wow!' exclaimed Tiana.

'See you already had one, you just had to realise it,' said Leila.

'Got your point,' smiled Tiana.

'I'm sure your "finding it" quest stopped you from sitting in the car too right?' asked Leila.

'Yes, actually it did stop me. The whole point of the entire thing was that I should do what I really feel in any situation . . . especially in those where I am under pressure. And that's what I did that night. I made a decision I believed in,' said Tiana.

'This has really helped you Tia. Everyone can feel this change in you. A good change. You have become so sure of yourself and so confident. I really wish that more girls should turn out like you,' said Leila.

'Like me? How?' asked Tiana.

'Girls who can say "no". By saying no they can save themselves from doing what they don't want to do,' said Leila.

'Thanks Leila! I feel so lucky to have you as my friend, said Tiana, smiling at her friend.

'Now stop buttering me!' said Leila.

'Tell me, how you are feeling now?' asked Tiana.

'My neck really hurts. And the cuts on my arms are painful but other than that, I think I will survive,' said Leila with a wink.

'Good. So I will see you in school. You take care of yourself,' said Tiana while hugging her friend.

'Bye Tia! I hope I get out of this hospital soon,' moaned Leila.

'You will, don't worry. Bye.'

Tiana reached home but she was thinking about what Leila had said. Had she really changed so much?

Tiana was not sure about change but while finding answers to the small questions on her list, she had discovered a lot of things about herself . . . things that she hadn't been consciously aware of earlier. It now dawned on her that she had known everything sub-consciously. Leila was actually right. She was never lost. She had just been out of touch with herself. Thanks to her efforts, that had changed. She knew what she wanted and it felt so good!

In the past two months, she had learnt to laugh at herself (thanks to Leila). She realised that she hated self-pity and because she would never pity herself, she would never give up on anything.

She wanted her friends and all the girls of her age to stand up and speak up for what they think is right. She wanted them to learn to say no and have self-control. Look what happened to her friends when they were not able to make a correct decision.

Tiana believed in helping the underdogs—people who did not have the guts to fight for themselves. She believed in encouraging them to respect themselves.

She did not like the two-faced stand and hypocrisy of the teachers. The way they encouraged the boys and at the same time discouraged the girls for the same things! Whatever happened to all those equality lessons they kept teaching students?

Tiana knew that she was a fighter. Not cocky but just enough to never get used as a doormat by people around her. No one could make her feel bad about herself.

Since the accident, she valued her friends more than ever. Now she understood just how important friends are in life.

Apart from all this, she knows the answers to all the questions on her list, except the last question . . . which could never have a permanent answer. Was she happy? For how long can someone stay happy? Surely never forever. The same went for Tiana. Of course, she is happy with life today. Her friends had survived a fatal accident. She had been saved from the same accident. It was sheer luck. She had been lucky to take the right decision at the right time and in the right way. It may or may not make sense. The bottom line is that today, she is very happy with her life. Who knows what will happen tomorrow?

One thing that was still on her mind was pink or black – the only question with two answers. Pink symbolises life, health, innocence, spring and happiness. Black is actually an absence of colour but it is still so beautiful (at least that's what she thought and believed in). It represents elegance, power and mystery. Why can't she pick one? After all, having a favourite does not mean that you don't like any thing else. You just like that particular thing a little more than the rest.

Just then her mom entered her room.

'I just wanted to see what you are up to,' said her mother, as she flopped down on Tiana's comfy corner bean bag.

'I am just finishing my packing. I don't want to forget anything,' said Tiana.

'Tia can I ask you something?' asked her mother.

'Of course mom.'

'What stopped you? How come you weren't in that car?'

Tiana hadn't really discussed the 'finding it' theory with her mother properly. Maybe, she thought, she should.

'Mom, remember I started this "finding it" thing during the winter holidays?' asked Tiana.

'Yes I do remember. You discovered that your favourite movie was *The Devil Wears Prada*, right?'

'Right,' said Tiana, and she went on to explain everything to her mother. Her mom was very impressed by the end of it.

'Wow Tia! You have really grown up. It must feel good to know that you saved yourself,' said her mother.

'It makes me feel great mom,' replied Tiana, 'I just need help with one little thing.'

'What is that?' asked her mother.

'It's the only question for which I have two answers.'

'Okay, what's the question?' asked her mother.

'My favourite colours. I am confused between pink and black,' said Tiana.

'Did it occur to you that you can have two favourite colours?' asked her mother.

'Yes, that did cross my mind. But then I realised that I have one favourite for everything else, then why not for colours?'

'That is because our favourite colours have something to do with our personalities too. Let's take an example – pink is just one side of your personality . . . the side which loves life, and wants to live it happily. Black is the other side of you, the stronger side which gives you hope and strength to see you through rough patches . . . and that's what has helped you in the past few days. Seeing such a horrible accident could have destroyed you psychologically. But you stayed strong. You did not crumble under that major disaster in your life. You still hoped for the best. You require strength for that. You need both the sides to live, Tia. There are so many beautiful colours. Why choose just one as your favourite?' finished her mother.

'Whoa! Where did all that come from?' Tiana was surprised. Her mother had just made life seem so simple to her.

'I don't know. I was just trying to help you honey.'

'You have done a good job ma,' said Tiana, and gave her mom a bear hug.

'Glad to help darling and even more to see the smile back on your face,' said her mother lovingly.

'My favourite colours are pink and black,' said Tiana proudly.

'My favourite colour is red,' joined her mother.

'That's Leila's favourite too,' said Tiana.

'How are Leila and Celia?' asked her mother.

'Leila says she will survive. Her neck was hurting but other than that, everything is okay.'

'Thank God! I was worried sick about all of them. But I know that they are not weaklings. They've got the spirit to face life head on.'

'Uh-huh!'

'Why? Aren't they?' asked her mother, a bit perplexed.

'No doubt they are. I just hope that they won't do something like this again,' said Tiana.

'Come on, everyone has learnt their lesson Tia.'

'Yes they have. I hope they won't forget it.'

'They won't,' said her mother.

'Have Dhruv and Daksh packed?' asked Tiana.

'I don't think so. I'm sure they're up to some mischief right now. Thanks for reminding me. I think I should go and check on them,' said her mother, getting up from the bed to leave.

'Mom.'

'Yes?'

'Thanks!'

Her mom kissed her on the forehead.

'I am proud of you Tiana!'

After her mom left, Tiana felt so much better. Her mom had solved her problem so easily. She was thanking her stars for having a mother who understood her. Just then, her mom re-entered her room.

'One of your friends has come to see you. Should I send him up?'

'Sure mom.'

A minute later, Tiana was surprised to see Karam enter her room. For the first time, her heartbeat gave a tiny skip.

'Hi Karam!'

'Hi Tia! I hope I'm not disturbing you?' asked Karam.

'Don't be silly! Of course not. In fact, I wanted to talk to you myself,' said Tiana.

'Everything okay?'

'Yes, but I am sorry that I haven't really managed to act like a good girlfriend yet,' said Tiana apologetically.

'Are you kidding me? So many things have been happening. They are issues that are much bigger than "us" and I just like you as you are. You don't have to act like anybody,' smiled Karam. He came a little closer and gently took her hand into his. Tiana could feel something that she hadn't experienced before. Was it butterflies fluttering in her tummy or bees buzzing in her head . . . she didn't know. All she knew was that this was a wonderful feeling and she was enjoying every second of it.

'Thanks.'

'By the way, how does a good girlfriend act?' laughed Karam. His eyes were glinting mischievously.

'I really don't know. Remember I am new to this?' Tiana laughed with him.

'I assure you that you are doing a very good job.'

They had a long chat after that. They talked about everything that was happening, and a teeny-weeny bit of sweet nothings too. Tiana couldn't believe that this was actually happening to her. Karam made Tiana feel so much better.

'I guess school will be murder. Everyone will want to hear about what had happened,' said Tiana.

'I know. Which reminds me that we are leaving tomorrow and I still haven't packed,' said Karam.

'You had better start then.'

'You are right. Good night T. I'll see you tomorrow.' With that, he gave her a bear hug and left the room.

∫

Just as Tiana had suspected, everyone in school grilled them with a volley of questions about the accident . . . a whole lot of them were especially reserved for Tiana, as she had been an eyewitness. Recalling the incident was the last thing she wanted to do and constantly being reminded about it wasn't helping. Even the teachers wanted to know everything. After getting their fair share of the latest news, they were happily clucking over kids being so notorious and drinking when they are not supposed to. They didn't even spare her from their questionnaires in the classroom. Hah! As if the questions in the text books were not enough!

'I am losing my nut,' said Lilly during lunch.

'I am sick of people staring at the cut on my face and then feeling sorry for me. That's so pathetic!' exclaimed Bella.

'You can't exactly blame them. It is kind of a big thing. Everyone is just curious,' said Karam. He was stroking his chin and acting like the voice of reason.

'It is big but for us, not them,' said Bella dramatically.

'Try telling them that,' scoffed Aryan.

Tiana sat quietly. This whole hullabaloo was irritating her a lot too. She had almost lost her cool and snapped at people a couple of times. But ultimately, she knew that Karam was right too. If people talked about Bella and Leila's hair, then it was only natural that they would want to know about an accident which almost killed them. Gossiping is a religion in any school. It's practised faithfully and all students are loyal devotees. So if people were going to talk about it, they might as well talk about the truth and not some senseless rumour. That is why she had been telling the truth to anyone who came up to ask her about what had happened. Of course, she tried to keep it as brief as possible but did not deny the gossip mongers their fair share of the information that, according to them, was absolutely necessary to know.

'What's up with you T?' asked Bella.

'Nothing really. I was just thinking,' replied Tiana, talking to Bella but staring into oblivion.

'Why are you telling them what happened? Isn't it irritating? I thought you didn't want to talk about it,' said Bella, with a confused look flitting across her face.

'It is hard to not talk about it when everyone around you is dying to know about it,' said Tiana.

'They should mind their own business,' grumbled Bella.

'But you know that they won't. Might as well tell them about it. Give them what they ask for and they'll lose interest soon,' said Tiana.

'Yup, Tia has a point there,' said Savera.

'Okay okay! Cut it out guys! At least we can avoid talking about it. We've started sounding like the news channels which keep flashing the same old "Breaking News" again and again just because they think the viewers love it!' said Karam.

'You are right,' agreed Bella.

After being frightened at the thought of sounding like news channels, the gang spent the rest of the lunch period in yapping away about bugging tests, teachers who get on their nerves and the Himalayan heaps of homework that they are subjected to. Tiana was happy to notice that her friends hadn't let the accident get an upper hand. They were still the same notoriously funny and adorable people who Tiana loved with all her heart. She missed Leila and Celia though. However the thought that they were recovering and would be back in school soon made her feel better.

In a way, the accident proved to be a lesson for a lifetime to all her friends as well as herself. Finally, her friends understood why Tiana had been pushing them to stop drinking. They learnt that being cool doesn't mean throwing away your life even before it started.

While everybody was busy chatting away, Tiana's mind was travelling down memory lane. She thanked fate for that one moment during English class in the previous year when she realised the need to drop the garb she was wearing and be herself. That's where her 'finding it' mission had started. Tiana smiled to herself while a voice inside her said 'Mission successful!' Her moment of exclusive glory (known only to herself) was suddenly interrupted when another bunch of kids came up to her with news thirsty eyes. Some things never change, thought Tiana and started explaining it to them all over again.

During the last class, Tiana realised that there was something she wanted to tell Bella. She wrote it on a piece of paper:-

Bella I just wanted to tell you that many times you remind me of 'Veronica Lodge' from the Archie comics.

–T.

She folded the paper and hissed at Bella. Bella looked in Tiana's direction. Tiana passed her the chit.

Bella read it and then looked at Tiana incredulously. Tiana shrugged her shoulders. Then Bella wrote something and slyly passed it back to Tiana. It said:-

Hehehe! Me too. I mean I started feeling the same a long time back. But none of you ever mentioned it. You've chosen a really funny time to tell me about it. Now I don't know how I'm gonna keep a straight face throughout the next 15 minutes of this sense-numbing class! Couldn't you wait for class to get over?

Tiana just smiled. The truth was she had waited long enough to tell Bella. She just couldn't wait for another fifteen minutes.

༄

That night, before sleeping, Tiana gave one last thought to everything that had happened in the last two months – her 'finding it' quest, the entire episode with Veer the creep, Leila and her stupid lie about going to Paris, Karam asking her out so suddenly, realising that she liked him after a century, and finally dating him. Oh my God, she still couldn't believe that she was actually dating him! And of course, the incident that she'll never forget – the accident which taught her the value of friends and life all over again.

Oh yes! The past couple of months had been quite a roller coaster ride but who ever said that life's roads were smooth and straight? Sure . . . it had a few bumps here, a few thorns there . . . but it also had quite a few stretches of smooth wide roads accompanied with flowers and birds on the sides. If it weren't for these hurdles and challenges, life would be so boring that it could give competition to their history class! It was always important to look forward to something in life . . . something positive, something happy and something you loved.

For now, she was looking forward to seeing Leila, Celia and Rehan again . . . fully recovered. After that, if nothing else, then . . . hmmmm . . . well, then she could always think about the dreaded month of March.

Oh yeah, the Boards.